a Dollop of Pride
&
a Dash of Prejudice

A Pride and Prejudice Variation Collection

Renata McMann
&
Summer Hanford

Cover by Summer Hanford

From Ashes to Heiresses © 2016
Epiphany with Tea © 2016
Miss Bingley's Christmas © 2016
Their Secret Love © 2020
Copyrights by Renata McMann & Summer Hanford
All rights reserved

ACKNOWLEDGEMENT

With special thanks to Nancy Simanek, Doris Studer and Karen Hanford.

Dear Reader,
After enjoying our story, consider signing up for our mailing list, where you will have the opportunity for free gifts, information about new releases and in person events, and more. Join us by visiting
www.renatamcmann.com/news/

By Renata McMann and Summer Hanford

After Anne
Their Secret Love
*A Duel in Meryton**
Love, Letters and Lies
The Long Road to Longbourn
*Hypothetically Married**
The Forgiving Season
The Widow Elizabeth
Foiled Elopement
Believing in Darcy
Her Final Wish
Miss Bingley's Christmas
Epiphany with Tea
Courting Elizabeth
The Fire at Netherfield Park
*From Ashes to Heiresses**
Entanglements of Honor
Lady Catherine Regrets
A Death at Rosings
Mary Younge
Poor Mr. Darcy
Mr. Collins' Deception
The Scandalous Stepmother
Caroline and the Footman
Elizabeth's Plight (The Wickham Coin Book II)
Georgiana's Folly (The Wickham Coin Book I)
The Second Mrs. Darcy

*available as an audio book

Collections:

A Dollop of Pride and a Dash of Prejudice:
Includes from above: *Their Secret Love*, *Miss Bingley's Christmas*, *Epiphany with Tea* and *From Ashes to Heiresses*.

Pride and Prejudice Villains Revisited – Redeemed – Reimagined A Collection of Six Short Stories.
Includes from above: *Lady Catherine Regrets*, *Mary Younge*, *Mr. Collins' Deception* and *Caroline and the Footman,* along with two the additional flash fiction pieces, *Mrs. Bennet's Triumph* and *Wickham's Journal*.

Georgiana's Folly & Elizabeth's Plight: Wickham Coin Series, Volumes I & II
Includes from above: *Elizabeth's Plight* and *Georgiana's Folly*.

Other Pride and Prejudice variations by Renata McMann
Heiress to Longbourn
Pemberley Weddings
The Inconsistency of Caroline Bingley
Three Daughters Married
Anne de Bourgh Manages
The above five works are collected in the book:
Five Pride and Prejudice Variations

Also by Renata McMann
Journey Towards a Preordained Time

Books by Renata McMann writing as Teresa McCullough

Enhancer Novels: Stand-alone novels in the same universe
Enhancers Campaign
The First Enhancer
The Pirates of Fainting Goat Island
The Enhancer with Meg Baxter

Bengt/Tian stories:
The Secret of Sanctua A Bengt/Tian novel
Kidnapped by Fae: a Bengt/Tian Short Story

Other stories:
The Slave of Duty with Meg Baxter
Lost Past

Thrice Born Series by Summer Hanford

Thrice Born Novels:
Gift of the Aluien
Hawks of Sorga
Throne of Wheylia
The Plains of Tybrunn
Shores of K'Orge

Songs of Rebellion Series:
Ballad of Discord

Under the Shadow of the Marquess Series:
The Archaeologist's Daughter
The Duke's Widow
The False Lady

Ladies Always Shoot First Half Hour Reads Series:
Captured by a Duke
To Save a Lord
One Shot for a Gentleman
Anything for a Lord

A Lord's Kiss Half Hour Reads Series:
Last Chance for a Lord
To Know a Lord's Kiss
A Lord's Dream
Deceived by a Lord

Installments in Scarsdale Publishing's Marriage Maker Series:
One Good Gentleman
My Lady of Danger
Rake Ruiner
Dreaming of a Gentleman
My Lady, My Siren
The Runaway Baroness
His Imaginary Courtship

TABLE OF CONTENTS

Epiphany with Tea 11
From Ashes to Heiresses 51
Miss Bingley's Christmas 93
Their Secret Love 119

Epiphany with Tea

A Christmas Tale

December 1822, Pemberley . . .

After nine years, Darcy knew Elizabeth well enough to guess she didn't consider their disagreement of the day before resolved. His first and most salient clue was the look she'd leveled on him after his previous day's declaration that he would not discuss the issue of Wickham's son further. It was the first time he'd made that sort of arbitrary declaration to Elizabeth and he'd regretted the words, his father's, as soon as they left his mouth. The glorious sight of her, shoulders back and eyes afire with emotion, was almost worth her anger, but he didn't truly enjoy provoking his wife or mirroring certain traits of his sire.

If her reaction yesterday hadn't been enough of an indication of her feelings, her absence that morning was. Normally, Elizabeth would appear, generally with one or both of their children in tow, as he was finishing dressing. From there, they would all go down to breakfast together, though little Jane, just three, generally stayed only a short time. Their son, Fitzwilliam, was eight now and took pride in exhibiting proper manners at the table, which, in turn, was a source of pride for Darcy. Today, however, Darcy dressed in suspicious silence, punctuated only by brief exchanges with a studiously bland valet.

Arriving in the breakfast parlor, Darcy found matters worse than expected. Instead of her usual place at his side, where she would sneak glances at his morning paper and converse with him on the topics, Elizabeth sat at the foot of the long table. She'd already served herself and sat straight backed, perched on the edge of her chair, slicing her food with deft strokes. She wore black. He knew it was out of respect for her recently deceased sister, Lydia, but Darcy still saw it as a grim omen. Though the color emphasized the fine quality of Elizabeth's complexion, he would have spared her the necessity of wearing it if he could.

"Good morning," Darcy said. He considered crossing the room to drop a kiss on her brow, but the somewhat savage and exceedingly efficient slicing warned him away. He crossed to the sideboard and served himself, motioning for one of the footmen to bring his coffee.

By the time Darcy took his seat, the silence from Elizabeth's end of the table was becoming acute. He took a sip of coffee, glancing about the room. His gaze lingered on the bow-bedecked evergreen boughs, festively placed over the windows and draping the mantel. He'd never confided it to her, but he loved that Elizabeth insisted on decorating so much of their home for the Yuletide. A secret part of him, harkening back to somewhere in his youth, drew a spark of wonder from the trappings of the season.

His perusal of the room coming full circle, he returned his gaze to his wife, whom he knew desired a continuation of their discussion on Wickham's son. "I believe this is where you supply a polite return greeting."

Elizabeth's eyes widened in a look of amusingly sincere innocence. "I take it, then, that having a good morning is a topic which we may discuss further?" She smiled sweetly.

Darcy cast another look around the room, this time noting the three footmen and two kitchen maids. "Would you excuse Mrs. Darcy and myself, please?" he said to the room at large.

They murmured ascent and shuffled out, not really hiding their disappointment. They would, he assumed, listen at the doors. At least that way they wouldn't actually witness his defeat, if indeed he suffered one, only overhear it.

"You cannot expect anyone else to take him, Darcy," Elizabeth said as soon as the door closed behind their staff.

Darcy suppressed a smile. One of the things he loved about his wife was her directness. "I can and I do. No one would fault me for not taking in George Wickham's son. Especially in view of my history with the man." Wickham had spread misconceptions about him, tried to elope with his sister when she was only fifteen, and cost him thousands of pounds. The last occurred shortly after he married Elizabeth, when Wickham ran off with Lydia but wouldn't marry her unless Darcy paid him a substantial amount. Wickham had known Darcy would pay to save his wife's sister from disgrace.

"Most people do not know the extent of your history with Mr. Wickham, and so would not weigh it when judging whether or not you should take in his son, but you cannot tell me that you truly care what most people think of your actions," she said, setting aside her silverware.

"Well, then, those who know me well enough to provide opinions which matter to me would not expect me to open my home to the boy." Surely, Elizabeth must understand that. He took another sip of coffee. "Think of our children."

"Our children?" She raised her eyebrows. "Surely you don't believe an eight-year-old boy is dangerous?"

"No, but he will be. If we take him in and raise him alongside Fitzwilliam, he will end up just as his father did. He'll grow to be useless, penniless, a seducer of gentlemen's daughters, a vagrant, and die in a duel over another man's wife three years after wedding." Or worse, Darcy added to himself.

"I suppose you believe he'll also grow up to attempt eloping with our daughter?" Elizabeth's tone was an equal mixture of amusement and exasperation.

"I do." Darcy set a firm look upon his face. He was resolved not to be swayed in this. He hadn't grieved the day Wickham died. He would not permit the man a postmortem foray into his life.

"Where, then, do you think my sister's son will go?"

Darcy didn't care, so long as it had nothing to do with his family, but he knew that was not the correct reply. "He shall live with your mother and Miss Mary. I'll increase their stipend. It will please them and give greater meaning to their lives."

"If there is anyone who would surely bring out the worst tendencies in the boy's nature, it is my mother. She is the perfect person to turn young George into all you fear he may become, and a terribly negligent parent. Perhaps if my father . . ." She trailed off, shrugging. As always when her late father was mentioned, sorrow flickered in her gaze.

Darcy, too, thought it was a shame Mr. Bennet had already left them. Though Darcy wasn't as confident in Mr. Bennet's parenting skills as Elizabeth seemed to be, no one was a more stimulating conversationalist, both on the too-rare occasions they'd met in person and by correspondence. Darcy still had all of his late father-in-law's letters, and sometimes referred to them for opinions, or simply to smile. He cleared his throat. "Miss Mary is there as well, to provide a sober influence."

"Yes, that's what the lad needs. My overly pious, insular sister spouting Bible verses she doesn't quite comprehend at him day after day."

"It will do him good," Darcy said, though he couldn't quite bring himself to believe any child would flourish under the neglect of Mrs. Bennet and the attention of Miss Mary.

Elizabeth leveled a look at him that spoke volumes on her opinion of the sincerity of his statement.

"Your sister Kitty was closest to Lydia," he offered.

"Kitty's health is increasingly precarious, rendering her nearly incapacitated most days, and her husband will never be promoted above lieutenant and has no family connections." Elizabeth narrowed her eyes at him. "Before you suggest it, you know he's too proud to permit you to buy a promotion for him."

"He wouldn't need to know who was responsible." Darcy knew there would be little doubt, though, that the promotion had been secured by him.

Elizabeth shook her head. "Darcy, you know we are the only choice. Would you send my sister's child to an orphanage?"

"There are the Bingleys, the Gardiners and the Philips." He leaned back in his chair, feeling slightly smug. Elizabeth couldn't possibly have a good reason why none of the three would suit.

"My Aunt and Uncle Gardiner have five children of their own to care for, and much fewer resources than we have. My Aunt Phillips would hardly be a better parent than my mother. In case you have forgotten, ever since Longbourn passed into Mr. Collins' care, my mother and Mary live two houses from the Phillips. You may as well subject the boy to Mother's care."

"You cannot have a reason your nephew can't go to the Bingleys." Darcy was confident enough in this to permit himself a celebratory grin.

Elizabeth's answering smile doused his. "Did I forget to tell you, then, that Jane is with child again?"

Darcy winced. Still, the Bingleys obviously enjoyed a large family, so why not add one more? He opened his mouth to say as much.

"Given that she's born two sets of twins already, and that she and Charles have six children already, I really don't feel we can ask it of them," Elizabeth said before Darcy could speak. Her smile fell. "You know Charles' investments haven't gone well," she said in a lower voice. "I don't want to put any more pressure on them. The strain is beginning to show."

Darcy was aware that Bingley was in some financial difficulties, but hadn't thought it anything significant. It wouldn't be like Elizabeth to fabricate, though. He frowned, reviewing recent interactions with his friend. If looked at through the lens of Elizabeth's words, he could construe some of Bingley's statements and an increase in the tension evident in his mien as indication that things were more dire than Bingley let on. "I didn't realize."

"He doesn't wish you to know, but Jane confided in me." Elizabeth stirred her tea, her expression contemplative. When she met his eyes again, her smile returned. "So, you see, we are the best choice."

"I do not see." Darcy grimaced at the slightly sullen edge to his words. "I will not have a young George Wickham in our home." He gentled his tone. "I am sorry Lydia died, especially so near Christmas, but you cannot ask me to welcome a repetition of the troubles inflicted on Georgiana and myself. What form of parent would I be if I willfully subjected our children to such trials?" He braced himself for her ire. Elizabeth was at least as strong willed as he was.

Her expression softened, much to Darcy's surprise. "You would be a good parent, because that is what you are." She pressed her lips into a contemplative line. "I believe the flaw here is in your basic assumption. Having refused to ever meet the boy, you do not know him. You assume he embodies the worst traits of both my sister and his father. You know I visited Lydia several times." She leaned forward, her expression earnest. "He's a good lad. You cannot condemn him for being his father's son. At least meet him. If life has taught me two things, one is that you must come to know someone before you deem yourself capable of judging them and the other is that you can't know a person based simply on their relations."

Darcy blinked. He took a sip of coffee. He knew Elizabeth's words were true, but it was George Wickham come again to intrude on the lives of Darcys. How could he condone that? Across the table from him, Elizabeth raised her teacup to her lips.

It was his mother's favorite set, he noted. Elizabeth preferred it. When they'd first wed, he'd given her every permission to replace it, if she so desired, but she hadn't. It was the same set, in fact, that his Aunt Catherine often used. The two, his mother and aunt, had both taken a liking to the pattern and commissioned them together, to match.

Seeing Elizabeth sitting across from him, cradling that delicate china cup with its expertly detailed roses, took Darcy back to the most important day in his life. The day Elizabeth Bennet agreed to be his.

Over Nine Years Earlier, April 1813, Rosings . . .

As usual, his Aunt Catherine was dominating the conversation. She was droning on about the weather, at what could only be considered an exhaustive length. She insisted it would rain that very evening. No one asked her what she based her forecast on. For his part, Darcy didn't care to know, or to prolong the experience by arguing.

His aunt's clergyman, Mr. Collins, seated to her right, didn't ask either. Instead, he agreed with her enthusiastically. That wasn't much worth noting, since he always agreed with her. Usually, Mrs. Collins was present to alleviate some of the tedium. She had a knack for turning the conversation to a new topic by asking Lady Catherine for advice. Today, however, Mrs. Collins was tending her visiting younger sister, who wasn't feeling well, and Darcy couldn't think of a single thing he was willing to ask Lady Catherine's advice on, although she would be happy to give advice on any topic, regardless of how much she actually knew about it.

Across from them, Darcy's cousin, Colonel Richard Fitzwilliam, appeared amused, though likely not for reasons their aunt would appreciate. Darcy glanced at Lady Catherine's daughter, Anne, seated near Richard. She wore an unreadable expression and Darcy didn't linger on it to attempt interpretation, or even spare a glance for her companion, Mrs. Jenkinson. Instead, he permitted his gaze to rest on the one person he wished most to observe, Elizabeth Bennet.

She sat, straight backed, on the edge of an overly-ornate settee, giving Lady Catherine her attention without the slightest trace of boredom or skepticism. It was one of the many things Darcy admired about Elizabeth. She was always polite. As he watched, she raised a delicate, rose-adorned teacup to her lips, taking a sip. From where he sat, he could observe she used the cup to hide a smile from his aunt, holding it before her until she regained control of her expression. Darcy admired the tactic.

Elizabeth's sparkling gaze flicked toward him, sharing her

amusement. It occurred to Darcy that, with her propensity for enlivened thought, she was likely entertained by how ludicrously his aunt was behaving. He ought to be offended. She should be more deferential. Elizabeth Bennet wasn't of a high enough station to be amused by his aunt.

Yet, in what other positive light could anyone regard the conversation? Lady Catherine was bullying, arbitrary and self-absorbed. Were she not a titled lady and his aunt, he would object to her behavior. One must either take up Elizabeth's tactic, be bored, or be affronted. Darcy generally elected boredom, but Elizabeth appeared to be having a much nicer time than he was.

It occurred to him, for all her inner merriment, Elizabeth likely did object to his aunt's behavior. His cousin Anne had detailed to him how Lady Catherine asked Elizabeth impertinent questions, which Elizabeth responded to with both politeness and spirit. Darcy wished he'd been witness to one such exchange. He could spend every day listening to Elizabeth's wit.

Elizabeth turned her attention back to his aunt, setting down the rose-adorned teacup. Darcy permitted his gaze to linger on her elegant profile, finding perfection there. He wondered if she had any notion of how he'd come to regard her? She must, for he took few pains to hide it. In light of that, her smile of moments ago must be viewed as encouraging. She must see him in a positive light, at the least.

Or must she? As his aunt droned on, Darcy mulled over his interactions with Elizabeth, looking for clues as to how she regarded him. He was perceived, he knew, as somewhat lofty. Did he appear to be similar to his aunt? Did others compare her obnoxious snobbishness with his reasonable recognition that he was better than most of those around him?

His gaze glided over Elizabeth's elegantly curved figure, wondering how she would react to his thoughts on himself. Would she argue with him and let him know if she considered him to have bad manners? Or, would she give him polite smiles and hide broader ones behind teacups?

If she did argue with him, would she be right to?

"Lady Catherine," a woman's voice said.

His musing interrupted, Darcy turned toward the sound. He was surprised to find Anne's companion was speaking. He couldn't recall a time the prim, drab looking woman had ever initiated conversation. Her role was not to do so, but to reply when spoken to.

"I'm giving my one month's notice," Mrs. Jenkinson continued. "Mr. Collins, I would like to post banns for Mr. Kendall and myself. I've written out our full names, marital statuses and parishes for you." Leaning forward, she offered Mr. Collins a piece of paper.

Mr. Collins' hands shot up, palms out as if staving off a physical onrush. He looked wildly at Darcy's aunt. Whatever guidance he expected to find wasn't forthcoming, for she wasn't looking at him. Her formidable attention was aimed at Mrs. Jenkinson.

"How dare you give notice in such a public location," Lady Catherine demanded, the many creases on her face pulled downward into a scowl. "To speak to me of such things before a room full of people, some of them not family, is unforgiveable."

Darcy admired his aunt's choice of criticism. He knew she disliked anyone to make a decision without her advice, especially a large one, and the news that Anne's companion wished to marry clearly upset her. She didn't belittle herself by attempting to claim the notice was insufficient or expressing anger toward Mrs. Jenkinson for wishing to leave. After all, a month was adequate time to interview replacements and what real care could a lady have over the loss of a household member who was little more than a servant? Instead, Lady Catherine was clever enough to give a reason for her antagonism that didn't degrade her station.

"I needed to speak to Mr. Collins about the banns," Mrs. Jenkinson said, her tone calm without being subservient.

"Who is this Mr. Kendall?" Lady Catherine glared about the room, causing Mr. Collins to cringe away from her.

Darcy's cousin, Anne, scooted forward in her chair, her expression determined. "You remember him, Mama. When his wife died two years ago, you told me to make a condolence visit."

"A visit?" Lady Catherine's angry look found a resting point in Anne. "You cannot expect me to believe one visit, years ago, led to this effrontery." She flipped a vein-etched hand toward Mrs. Jenkinson.

"Of course not," Anne said. "We've visited regularly since then."

"I didn't ask you to go there more than once." Lady Catherine's scowl deepened. "Why didn't you stop going before it got out of hand?"

"I don't see it as out of hand," Anne said. "I see it as two people finding happiness in marriage."

Lady Catherine glared at her daughter. Anne, to Darcy's surprise, did not shrink or look away. She bore her mother's wrathful expression with pursed lips and steady eyes. Around their locked gazes, a strained silence took hold of the parlor. The only sound was the slight rustling of fabric as Mr. Collins looked frantically from mother to daughter and back again.

"Mrs. Jenkinson, I hope you will be very happy," Elizabeth said, her warm tone setting them all free. "I think it delightful that you are getting married."

"Yes," Richard said. He cleared his throat. "Please introduce me to Mr. Kendall when you have the opportunity. I would like to congratulate him. He's a lucky man."

Lady Catherine awarded the room another of her formidable scowls. "But what are you going to do without Mrs. Jenkinson?" she demanded of Anne. "I cannot believe you permitted this to happen. Are you daft? You know you can't be alone and it's terribly difficult to find anyone who suits you."

What was terribly difficult, Darcy knew, was to find anyone who could tolerate life with his aunt. Anne, for her part, was easy enough to get along with.

"I am not daft, Mother," Anne replied. She shrugged, dropping her gaze to the floor. "I'm sure we'll find someone who suits, but until then I will simply have to be companionless."

"You? Impossible. How will you live? What will you do with yourself?"

Darcy winced at his aunt's incredulous tone. Anne was a grown woman, not a child of six.

"I don't know, Mother, but I am going to find out." The expression Anne lifted from her contemplation of the carpet was resolute, much to Darcy's surprise.

"Impossible," Lady Catherine snapped. "I won't have it. Someone of your station should not be without a companion. How could you show your face anywhere?"

"We don't go anywhere," Anne muttered.

"This is not to be borne," Darcy's aunt continued over Anne's words. "I will not have a daughter of mine belittled by people thinking she can't find a suitable companion." Lady Catherine pursed her lips. "I wonder . . ." Her gaze traveled the room again. Beady eyes skimmed over Elizabeth with a grimace, and Richard in a contemplative way, before reaching Darcy. "Well, there is a simple solution. We can get a special license and you and Darcy can marry before Mrs. Jenkinson does." She reached for a bell. "I'll write to the archbishop immediately and the two of you can be married by—"

Darcy felt a familiar anger flare up inside him, made ten times stronger than usual by the knowledge that Elizabeth was witnessing his aunt ordering him about and trying to force him to marry Anne. "No," he said in his firmest tone.

Darcy had never considered giving in to his aunt's wish that he marry Anne, and his opposition to the idea had only grown along with his regard for Elizabeth. He set his jaw firmly, in the way he recalled his father doing when his mind was made up. It was time to set his aunt straight, once and for all, before Lady Catherine discovered his attachment to Elizabeth and took whatever mad steps she would be driven to. "I will never, under any circumstances, for any reason, marry Anne. You will give up this idea here and now."

His aunt's eyes went wide. She wet her lips, appearing nervous. Darcy couldn't recall her ever looking even a little unsure before. She must have recognized his father's tone, for he'd been even more formidable than Lady Catherine. "You must marry Anne," she cried in a surprisingly pleading voice. "How else can I have a Fitzwilliam inherit Rosings?"

"I'm not a Fitzwilliam, but a Darcy. Anne is as much a Fitzwilliam as I am. Besides, I don't believe in first cousins marrying," he added in a less strident voice, casting Anne an apologetic look as it occurred to him how insulting his vehemence was.

"No, Anne isn't a Fitzwilliam, and she isn't your cousin, not by blood at any rate," Lady Catherine cried, surging to her feet. "I am to hold Rosings for her until she marries, and it will be to a Fitzwilliam. I did not endure half a lifetime wed to Sir Lewis only to lose Rosings to another family." As quickly as she'd risen, Lady Catherine flung herself back into her chair, blinking rapidly, a sheen of unshed tears brightening her hawkish eyes.

It was the first time in Darcy's life he could recall having to consciously close his mouth because it was hanging open. A quick glance showed similar astonishment on the other faces in the room, even Anne's. Lady Catherine smoothed her skirts, a nervous gesture, but her expression turned hard.

"What did you just say?" Richard croaked into the silence.

"I am Sir Lewis de Bourgh's second wife." Lady Catherine tilted her chin to an arrogant angle. "He married beneath himself, in a hurried and quiet way, to a woman named Smith with no family or connections. She died in childbirth days after the wedding. He married me six months later."

Darcy could only stare at his aunt in shock.

"I've heard the occasional rumor . . ." Richard's low voice trailed off.

"Which I am sure you subdued." Lady Catherine's words were more an order than a question.

"Aggressively, if needed," Richard said, his syllables drawn out, revealing his shock. "Because I thought they were lies. I once dueled a man over it. I left him crippled."

"As he deserved for spreading such filth," Lady Catherine snapped.

Darcy wrenched his gaze from his aunt to look at Richard, whose face was white and pinched.

"She's not your daughter?" Mr. Collins blurted out.

"She is my daughter. She has known no other mother, and I have had no other child."

"How could you keep this from me?" Anne said, her voice cracking with the strain of her emotions.

Richard turned toward her, holding out a hand, which she clasped.

"There was no point in confusing you. You are too much like your mother already. She, by all reports, was meek and ineffectual. Not even strong enough to withstand bearing a child. Not the stuff a lady is made of. Your father was lucky he escaped the union so quickly."

Mrs. Jenkinson gasped, stifling the sound with her palm. Darcy raised his eyebrows. Had his aunt just implied it was a boon Anne's mother had died? He glanced at Elizabeth, to weigh her reaction, but her expression was carefully blank.

"My mother, Miss Smith," Anne repeated, sounding as stunned as Darcy felt.

"Yes, Miss Anne Smith." A hard smile curved Lady Catherine's lips. "People assume I named you after my sister, but your father named you after your mother. Anne is a common name and people are simpletons." She shrugged. "You're insecure enough being the granddaughter of an earl. Would it have helped you to know you're really the granddaughter of a miller?"

"It might have," Anne said. "It might explain why I could never fit."

"A de Bourgh doesn't need to fit," Lady Catherine said. "The world fits itself to a de Bourgh."

"Not to me," Anne whispered.

Darcy shook his head. What arrogance his aunt had. To keep such things from Anne, to applaud Richard for wounding a man for speaking the truth, as if doing so was honorable, and to expect the entirety of the world to adjust itself to fit with her wishes. It was unreasonable. It was tyrannical. It went beyond pride.

Darcy had always assumed his aunt wished him to marry Anne because she wanted to know her daughter was well cared for, but it seemed that was untrue. Did Lady Catherine even care for Anne? Was Rosings her only true love? "You want me to marry Anne not because of any pact between you and my mother, but because you want Rosings to go to your sister's grandchild?"

"When you were born, your mother and I speculated that if I ever had a daughter, the two of you might marry. When I married Sir Lewis, she knew about his child and we took it as confirmation for our earlier speculation. I've worked hard to make Anne into the prefect wife for you, Darcy. Your mother may be gone, but I've spent my life doing this for you. It's best for the Fitzwilliam line, for Rosings, and for you. Now that you know the truth, and that your outlandish objection to cousins wedding is moot, I'm sure you see that you must marry her."

Anne let out a small sound, somewhere between a hiccup and a sob. Though Richard still held one of her hands, Darcy could see the other trembled where it rested on the arm of her chair. He understood the inclination, for it seemed as if his gut has been rattled out of place. Elizabeth, in contrast, sat so still, he thought the others may have forgotten she was there.

He turned back to his aunt, realizing she was watching him through narrowed, assessing eyes. "I do not see any such thing. My marrying Anne may have seemed like a possibility when you were speculating with my mother, but it is not a possibility to me."

"But I have overcome your objections. I'm offering you Rosings, you fool. Take it."

"Forgive me for interrupting," Richard said before Darcy could formulate a reply through the anger her arrogance sparked in him. "If you want Rosings to be inherited by someone related to you, Aunt Catherine, how about if I marry Anne?"

"No," Elizabeth said, speaking for the first time.

Darcy turned to her, aghast. Could she have feelings for Richard? Yes, they'd been cordial to one another but . . . Darcy's hands curled into fists.

"Colonel Fitzwilliam, I'd thought better of you than this," Elizabeth continued. "Miss de Bourgh is of age. You don't court her mother, but her. That is no way to propose marriage. Whoever her mother is, Miss de Bourgh deserves better from you, all of you." She ended her speech with a look toward Lady Catherine, who glowered back.

Richard blinked several times, obviously surprised. "Well, yes, I know that, but this is not a romantic proposal. Anne realizes that, I'm sure. What must be made clear is that we get on well enough and that I meet the requirement of being a Fitzwilliam."

Anne yanked her hand from Richard's, her expression revealing hurt.

"Her stepmother's requirement, not hers," Elizabeth said. She shook her head. "A woman deserves better than a man who delivers words of logic to a parent, or even to her. She deserves at least a modicum of passion. Such a decision cannot be made wholly on logic. It would be better to remain unwed for all time than to submit to an emotionless union." She darted a glance toward Mr. Collins, whom Darcy had forgotten, and colored slightly.

"This is not a topic for you, you impertinent girl," Lady Catherine snapped. "Speak again and I shall ask you to leave, all of you. Darcy, you will marry Anne. You cannot have a worthy objection."

Darcy ignored his aunt, his attention on Elizabeth. Suddenly, everything came into place. For days, he'd been arranging the details of his feelings for Elizabeth in his thoughts, sorting the objections and obstacles into neat categories and applying logic to positives and negatives alike. Upon realizing he actually intended to propose to her, he'd planned to lay them out to her as he had to himself. He'd assumed a woman of her intelligence would appreciate a clear delineation of both sides of his argument for her hand. Listening to her defense of Anne, though, he realized that was obviously not the way to propose. "Let me show you," he said to Richard.

Richard nodded, his expression bemused.

Instead of going to Anne, as Darcy imagined the others expected, he got down on one knee in front of Elizabeth. Reaching out, he captured the rose-adorned teacup and saucer she cradled loosely, his fingers brushing hers as he took the porcelain dishes and set them aside. Her eyes widened and he wondered if she realized he was serious in his actions. He predicted the others in the room did not.

Looking up into her lovely visage, Darcy took a steadying breath. "Miss Bennet, I ardently love and admire you. Your beauty is unrivaled, your wit unmatched. I've seen you use tact with people who lack it, and admired you for it. I watched your loving care of your sister when she was ill." He noted how her eyes softened at the mention of her sister. Encouraged, he sought about for something more he could say about her family. "Your father is clever and your mother hospitable. Your older sister is kind, your middle sister is industrious in her pursuit of accomplishments, and your younger two sisters are cheerful and friendly." There. That should cover that. Did he have to say something about her uncle the attorney and his wife? No. He'd already used hospitable for her mother, and he couldn't think of anything else nice to say about them.

Elizabeth regarded him with raised brows, her delicate lips round with surprise, but it was the amusement dancing in her gaze that stabbed him. She was surprised, yes, but not by the ardor of his proposal, only by his behavior, which she obviously took as a joke. Any thought he'd had that she knew about his courtship was quenched.

Starting to feel foolish, Darcy realized he needed to cover his emotions before anyone saw the truth in them. Still on one knee, he turned to Richard. "Stress the positives," he said in a conversational tone. "You may not love Anne, but you like her." He got up, dusting off his knees. "Try." He couldn't bring himself to look at Elizabeth and the laughter in her eyes.

Richard stood, turning to face Anne. Hesitantly, he lowered himself to one knee, looking up at her. "Marry me. I am a poor soldier with no hope of more than a soldier's life."

"Talk about her," Darcy said.

"Don't talk at all and stand up this instant," Lady Catherine said. "I will not have my drawing room turned into a stage where you make absurd and insincere proposals."

Darcy's face heated. He glanced at Elizabeth, who was looking pityingly at Richard. He realized he shouldn't have stood. This was his opportunity. He'd started his proposal and he would finish it. He couldn't let things stand as they were, for that would be ruin. After all, what man could hope to recover from a botched proposal?

Squaring his shoulders, Darcy held out a hand to Elizabeth. "Miss Bennet."

She turned to him, taking in his proffered hand with surprise. Her expression curious, she placed her palm in his and he pulled her to her feet. He didn't release her, but instead brought her fingers to his lips.

"Miss Bennet," he repeated, lowering but not relinquishing her warm hand. He leaned closer, hoping his eyes expressed what was in his heart. "I wish your sister were here, so I could use your Christian name freely, even if I would still have to put the word Miss in front of it." He lowered his voice, not to keep the others from hearing, but because the intimacy of his feelings demanded it. "I say it in my mind over and over, savoring every syllable. Sometimes, to vary it, I use the nickname your family uses."

She appeared truly shocked now, all amusement gone from her gaze. The hand he held trembled slightly, and he reached for her other, clasping both between them.

"I want you to be by my side as I go through life. I want you to be the mother of my children. I want to see you holding our child in your arms. I want to show you the beauties of Pemberley. I want you to be there to correct me when I am wrong and to encourage me when I am right. Elizabeth Bennet, will you marry me?"

"This is going too far," Lady Catherine cried.

From the corner of his eye, Darcy could see his aunt was on her feet, her face a deep red, but he didn't take his gaze from Elizabeth's. Hers searched his face, touching on it with an intensity he could almost feel. Her slender fingers tightened about his.

"You're serious," she breathed.

"He is not serious," Lady Catherine shouted.

Mr. Collins appeared beside Darcy's aunt, his gangly arms fluttering about. "Cousin Elizabeth, come away from Mr. Darcy this instant. Release his hands. How dare you behave in such a vulgar way in front of Lady Catherine de Bourgh." The clergyman sounded as if he might collapse into tears.

"You brought this fiend of a woman into my home," Lady Catherine screeched, turning her anger on Collins.

"Enough," Darcy said, relinquishing one of Elizabeth's hands to face them. "Leave your lackey be, Aunt Catherine. I met Miss Bennet long before she came to Rosings."

Lady Catherine was scowling at him, her chest heaving with the force of her anger. Mr. Collins cringed at her side, somehow crinkling his tall frame into something shorter than she was. Behind them, Mrs. Jenkinson sat in the corner looking perfectly composed, while Richard and Anne both wore surprised expressions.

"We are making a scene," Darcy said, his tone quelling.

"We? You and Richard are making a scene. You are making jokes of yourselves," Lady Catherine snapped.

"If we are, then I am not finished," Richard said.

Darcy looked past Elizabeth to see Richard turn back to Anne, before whom he still knelt. "Anne, I can't make an impassioned speech as Darcy did. I'm a simple man. I'm an honest man, as you know. I've never thought of you in a romantic way, but I can begin doing so. I think there is a great comfort in wedding someone you know well, and know you get along with. Many marriages don't have passion. Many do, only to see it flicker out and leave nothing of substance in its wake. We already have the substance, you and I. That will carry us through all of the years, come what may, and, I dare to hope, it will see us happy." Richard grinned. "Also, I am willing to sign a marriage contract which gives you half of the net income from Rosings and all of your dowry, and I believe you should have the freedom to spend what is yours."

Lady Catherine threw up her hands, retaking her seat, arms folded across her chest and her face averted. Mr. Collins all but fell into his chair. Anne looked down at Richard, a deep line marring her brow as she considered him. Finally, she turned toward Darcy and Elizabeth.

"How am I meant to respond?" she asked, clearly addressing Elizabeth.

Elizabeth shot Darcy an inscrutable look, sparking worry in him. She turned back to Anne. "There are basically three choices. You can say yes. In your case, I would make it clear you do so contingent on the financial arrangements, since Colonel Fitzwilliam offered them and as you have much at stake."

She fell silent, glancing at Darcy again. With a murmur of apology, Richard pulled himself to his feet, retaking the chair beside Anne. He held out a hand. She took it without looking, seeming almost unaware she did so. Richard, Darcy realized, had been looking after Anne for a long time. True, only when he was visiting, but he visited often. More often than Darcy did.

"What are the other two choices?" Anne prompted.

"You can say you need to think it over, in which case you would politely offer a time limit. The time limit shouldn't be more than a day or two. You can't expect to hold him hanging." Elizabeth pursed her lips. "Or, you can say no. In that case, you should thank him for the honor of his proposal. It is an honor, even if both gentlemen went about it in an exceedingly odd way and keep taking liberties with our persons."

She tugged slightly and Darcy quickly released her hand, feeling a bit ill-used by the reprimand. Then again, she hadn't said yes yet, so he had no right to her person. Did her removal of her hand signal she would decline? A harsh weight settled in the pit of his stomach.

"What do you plan to do?" Anne asked.

Darcy noticed Anne didn't reclaim her hand. He cast a sideways look at Elizabeth, catching the pitying glance she was directing toward him. She was going to say no, he realized. He couldn't permit it. Elizabeth, he'd come to appreciate, had a stubborn streak. If he let her refuse him, it would be difficult to change her mind. He shook off the panic trying to freeze his tongue, speaking before she could. "She is going to do the same thing you are, Anne. She is going to listen in private, voice whatever objections she has, explain her motives, ask me any questions, and then make an informed decision. This is too important to do without thought." Lady Catherine let out a derisive snort, but Darcy ignored her, pressing on. "Anne, you've known Richard all of your life, but you probably have questions for him as well, in light of this possible change in your relationship." He turned to face Elizabeth, proffering his arm. "Come, Miss Bennet, let's walk in the shrubbery. I'm sure Anne and Richard can find a place for their conversation as well."

"None of you will walk anywhere," Lady Catherine said, but her tone was more peevish than angry. "You shall drop this nonsense and remain here."

Her expression thoughtful, Elizabeth accepted Darcy's arm.

"Anne," Richard said, standing. "Would you care to walk in the garden with me?"

"She would not care to." Lady Catherine's tone had regained some of its earlier vehemence. "Anne, I am still your mother. I raised you. You will remain in your seat."

"I would love to walk in the garden, Richard, thank you," Anne said, rising to take the arm he offered. "Or should I call you Colonel Fitzwilliam, as we are not truly cousins?" She shot Lady Catherine a venomous look.

"I would prefer Richard."

Lady Catherine raised a slightly shaking hand to her brow. "This is some kind of inexplicable joke. You have all conspired to make light of me."

Ignoring his aunt, Darcy led Elizabeth from the room. Behind them, he could hear Anne and Richard following.

"But it's going to rain." Mr. Collins protest followed them down the hall.

Present Day, December, Pemberley...

Elizabeth watched Darcy over her teacup, employing the delicate porcelain to conceal her smile as his gaze grew abstract. After ten happy years, she knew that look well. He was evaluating, thinking, considering. It was a small victory, for his evaluation may not come out in her favor. She knew, though, that she'd chosen her words well. Darcy was as aware as she of the pitfalls of judging someone without knowing them.

She understood Darcy's reluctance, likely better than any other person could. Mr. Wickham had overshadowed Darcy his entire childhood. He'd been a charming, pretty boy and a favorite of Darcy's father. Elizabeth had never met the previous master of Pemberley, and never confided her feelings about him to her husband, but she didn't quite like the man. What sort of father made his shy, serious son feel he wasn't as good as the brash, amiable child of another?

Elizabeth's smile grew. It amused her that she could speak of not judging people one wasn't familiar with, her manner infused with righteousness, and then condemn the late Mr. Darcy in her thoughts. Still, in a way she was familiar with him, through his children. Of course, in that case, she must love him, for Darcy and Georgiana were wonderful people, with firm moral characters, and who brought great happiness into her life.

Composing her features, Elizabeth lowered her cup. Darcy was well into thought now. She could see it in his abstract gaze. She hoped he would agree to meet young George, at least. He was, as she'd said, a good lad. He showed little of his parents' wildness and was always polite and happy to see Elizabeth when she visited. In truth, he reminded her more of her sister Jane than of Lydia or Wickham, though in his features he somewhat resembled his father.

She studied Darcy's face, even more handsome than when they'd married. While she feared the passing years were adding lines to hers, though most were lines of laughter, they'd merely added greater consequence to Darcy's visage. As she watched, his lips turned up slightly in a smile, and she couldn't help but mirror it.

Elizabeth ran an idle finger over the roses circling her teacup. She used the set often, and had taken special care to ensure it was out today. It was her favorite, for it reminded her of one of the happiest days of her life, the one when she'd realized she loved Darcy. She had no way to know if it brought the same memories to him, but the roses always invoked a feeling of joy in her heart, and she'd wanted that today.

Retrieving her silverware, she took a bite of her now cooled food, turning her gaze out the window. She loved the grounds of Pemberley, which were stunning even now, snow kissed. Perhaps, if the day went well, she would take the children for a walk later, and Darcy would join them. He'd promised to throw snowballs with their son, and make a snowman with little Jane, and he would. Darcy always kept his promises. It was one of the things she loved about him.

Her eyes tracing the white-iced branches, Elizabeth's mind turned to a different walk, on a different grounds. It was spring then. A beautiful, perfect spring day. A day on which she'd been misjudging Darcy terribly, and it hadn't rained.

Over Nine Years Earlier, April 1813, Rosings . . .

Elizabeth walked through the grounds of Rosings in silence, her hand resting lightly on Mr. Darcy's arm. She was waiting for him to tender an apology for involving her in his family's tumult, or to beg her forgiveness for subjecting her to his charade. Perhaps she would even tease him a bit by pretending she believed his proposal.

She glanced at him askance, taking in his serious expression. He didn't look as if he'd appreciate being teased. In truth, the idea didn't appeal to her. His proposal had seemed much to sincere to make light of.

Yes, it had felt very sincere and, for a moment, she'd believed. Then logic had asserted itself. Mr. Darcy's proposal couldn't be an honest one. He barely knew her, or she him. She shook her head. The very idea was ridiculous. The grand Mr. Darcy, who found her only tolerable, would never lower himself to proposing marriage to her, a mere country girl. More than likely, he'd felt secure in making her play a part in his little drama because he imagined she would know there was no possibility he was sincerely interested in someone as low as he saw her to be.

Still, he had proposed, and before witnesses. Elizabeth would never ruin both of their lives by forcing him into a union, but she would use his imprudent behavior to some advantage. She had before her the perfect opportunity to improve the circumstances of her friend Mr. Wickham, for surely Mr. Darcy owed her something by way of apology for his behavior. Adopting a casual bearing she said, "I understand the living willed to Mr. Wickham was given to someone else. Don't you feel he should be compensated for the loss?"

"You mean by more than the three thousand pounds he already received?" Mr. Darcy asked, frowning slightly.

"Three thousand pounds," she exclaimed, momentarily taken aback. Could that possibly be true? "He never mentioned receiving that."

"I don't have the document he signed giving up the living with me, of course, but Colonel Fitzwilliam knows about it. Please ask him."

Elizabeth stopped, pulling away from him. She turned to scrutinize his face. He appeared sincere enough, but this was a man who had, moments ago, put on a very convincing show of asking for her hand in marriage. "I don't believe you."

His frown deepened. "Then I repeat, ask Colonel Fitzwilliam. I believe he's in the garden." Mr. Darcy turned and headed toward the garden, walking rapidly. Elizabeth kept up with him, her certainty that he was lying diminishing in the face of his assurance.

They found Colonel Fitzwilliam and Miss de Bourgh seated opposite each other on a set of low stone benches enshrouded by an arbor of climbing roses. It was obvious they were conversing, but broke off before Elizabeth and Mr. Darcy drew near enough to hear, turning to watch their approach. Miss de Bourgh looked back and forth between them, a line of confusion marring her brow.

"Miss Bennet, Darcy," Colonel Fitzwilliam greeted, standing as they drew near. "May we be of some service to you?"

"Richard, please tell Miss Bennet why Mr. Wickham didn't receive the family living my father willed him," Mr. Darcy said, his lack of preamble conveying more disquiet than his expression did.

"Because he received three thousand pounds to give it up," Colonel Fitzwilliam said promptly, aiming an assessing look at Elizabeth. "It was Mr. Wickham's idea."

She didn't know what to say. Though she didn't want to believe Mr. Wickham had so grossly misled her, or that she may have so vastly misunderstood Mr. Darcy, Colonel Fitzwilliam seemed sincere as well. Furthermore, he'd given the same information Mr. Darcy had, without prompting.

"Thank you. I'm sorry to interrupt." Mr. Darcy bowed to his cousins before turning to face Elizabeth, proffering his arm.

"Then, when Darcy refused to give Mr. Wickham the living after the incumbent died, he tried to persuade Darcy's sister to elope with him," Miss de Bourgh said before Elizabeth could decide if she wished to take the offered arm or not.

Mr. Darcy and Colonel Fitzwilliam both spun to face Miss de Bourgh, wearing matching expressions of shock.

Miss de Bourgh, however, was looking at Elizabeth, her face serious. "That was last year, when Georgiana Darcy was only fifteen."

"How do you know that?" Colonel Fitzwilliam asked, his words clipped.

"She told me."

If anything, both men appeared even more surprised.

Miss de Bourgh shrugged her narrow shoulder. "Well, she had to talk to someone. You and Darcy weren't talking to her about it, except to repeatedly tell her it wasn't her fault. She needed someone to sympathize with her, not tell her she was too young to be responsible for her actions."

Mr. Darcy's expression turned hard. "You will not go about sharing Georgiana's shame, Anne."

"You're being the fool Mother labeled you, Darcy," Miss de Bourgh said with more spirit than Elizabeth would have credited her. "I'm not going about it. I'm telling the woman you hope to marry, because she doesn't like you much and a large part of that dislike stems from her erroneous perception of Mr. Wickham and his relationship with you."

It was Elizabeth's turn to be shocked. "I beg your pardon?"

"Mrs. Collins often needs someone to talk with too," Miss de Bourgh said, her expression smug.

Elizabeth had no notion of what to say to that, at least not to the three people she was with. She could think of several things to say to Charlotte, none of them very courteous.

Miss de Bourgh turned back to Colonel Fitzwilliam. "Now, Richard, I believe you were telling me about why you should resign your commission."

"Ah, yes, right," Colonel Fitzwilliam said. Giving them an apologetic shrug, he retook his seat.

His face a mask, Mr. Darcy offered his arm once more. This time, Elizabeth took it. With long strides, he led them back to their original path. They walked in silence while Elizabeth attempted to comprehend Miss de Bourgh's and Colonel Fitzwilliam's words. Not only was Mr. Wickham a cad and Mr. Darcy not a brute, but, as unbelievable as it seemed, Mr. Darcy had obviously meant his proposal.

Elizabeth drew in a deep breath. Apparently, she owed Mr. Darcy an apology. "I'm sorry. I misjudged you."

"It was understandable. You did not know me and had only Wickham's words on the subject. I realize he is charming." He raised his face, appearing to study the sky. "Anne said Wickham was a large part of why you don't like me." Did she imagine the pain in his voice as he spoke? "What other parts are there?"

"I'd rather not say. No good can come of it." Even had she still thought Mr. Darcy the monster Wickham painted him as, there was no reason to torment him.

"Miss Bennet, I don't mean to give up my pursuit of you quite so easily," Mr. Darcy said, to her surprise. "I believe honesty is our only course, and am willing to try it even if it hurts my chances that you will accept my proposal. If I confess to doing something that cannot at all please you, will you share your grievances so I may have a chance to refute them?"

Elizabeth mulled over his words, turning her head to contemplate his profile. Her first thought was to refuse to discuss the matter further. She did not care for Mr. Darcy and therefore did not wish to marry him. But what if her dislike was woven of figments, as Miss de Bourgh implied? If so, he deserved fresh evaluation. If his proposal was not an act, then it seemed, astonishing as it was, that he did love her.

He loved her enough to propose to her, in spite of her lack of connections or funds. To propose to her before his relations, and bare his feelings for all to see, even his tyrannical aunt. Elizabeth had spoken to Miss de Bourgh of the passion a man should bring to a union. Mr. Darcy had shown her that passion, in spades.

Not to mention, when one wasn't busy abhorring him, he was rather handsome. Tall, too, with a fine frame. Elizabeth felt her face heat slightly and she dropped her gaze to the path. "Assuming your confession is of a nature comparably momentous to mine, I agree. We shall trade, but as this is your proposal, you will not mind going first."

He smiled slightly. "I will mind, but I will also agree." He cleared his throat, tugging at his cravat. "I discouraged Mr. Bingley from proposing to your eldest sister."

"I suspected as much," she said, not masking the anger in her tone. "Why?"

"The most cogent reason is that I didn't think she loved him."

"She did." Anyone who knew Jane well could see that.

"She seemed, well, too serene to be in love."

Elizabeth clenched her fists, trying to keep control of her anger. He didn't speak again, apparently waiting on her. Though thoughts of Jane's sorrow twisted her heart, Elizabeth took a steadying breath. She would not fall into the trap of judging too quickly yet again. She cast Mr. Darcy another appraising look.

He said Jane had seemed too serene. Is that how her sister appeared to others? Elizabeth had spoken with Charlotte about that very issue. They'd discussed how little Jane showed her feelings. Charlotte's opinion seemed, in fact, to mirror Mr. Darcy's, and Charlotte did know Jane well. Not as well as Elizabeth knew her sister, but then, no one did. She finally said, "You have a point. You said most cogent. What were your other reasons?"

"One reason was a mistaken one. I realized that today. Who knew that tea at Rosings would bring such enlightenment?" This last he said in a low voice, as if speaking to himself, his gaze still turned upward. "I realized, for the first time, that most people justifiably dislike Lady Catherine. I could list her faults, but you probably know them better than I do. I don't see them, because she is family. I could see the faults in your family because they weren't mine. It was only when I seriously considered marrying you that I found those faults forgivable. I now realize that if I marry you, your family will become mine, and I will accept them as I do Lady Catherine. Before I fell in love with you, I could not accept your relatives, and I thought Mr. Bingley would dislike them enough that any chance at finding happiness with your sister would be ruined by them. Clearly, I was wrong in that. If loving you permits me to feel acceptance toward your family, Bingley would have no trouble doing so. He is a much more accepting person than I am. I'm certain he would come to care for them."

It took all of Elizabeth's concentration not to trip over her own feet during Mr. Darcy's speech. Did he realize he'd said he loved her? Twice. Her cheeks felt as if they were on fire, though her feelings were in too much turmoil for her to know if it was embarrassment or some other emotion that burned there. She was glad he wasn't looking at her. She tried to marshal her thoughts, realizing she needed to respond. "That seems convoluted," she finally said.

"That is why I almost didn't understand it myself," Mr. Darcy replied.

Elizabeth could say little to that, as she still wasn't sure she understood. All she truly comprehended from his monologue was that he loved her, and he cared for her family. Mr. Darcy loved her?

"The last reason was Mr. Bingley," Mr. Darcy said. He shook his head. "Bingley falls in and out of love on a regular basis. I thought that when he stopped seeing your sister, he would stop caring for her, proving his feelings were as fleeting as ever. She seems too kind a person to saddle with a man of fleeting affection." He shrugged, the muscles of his arm rippling under her hand. "I was wrong on that, too. He hasn't been involved with anyone else since being parted from your sister. Though he hasn't said anything, it seems increasingly as if Bingley is pining for her. Are you certain she loved him?"

"Yes," she said, still saddened by what he'd done, though her anger had dimmed with each of his reasons.

"Regardless of how you answer my proposal, I will write him this evening and tell him I was wrong to think Miss Bennet didn't love him."

"That is generous." Most men wouldn't admit they were wrong, especially in writing. Then, she was beginning to understand that Mr. Darcy was not most men.

"It is the least I can do, though also the most, I think, for the matter is not truly in my hands, but Bingley's and your sister's. It is possible nothing will come of it. His feelings may have changed since last I saw him or, if he does attempt to pursue her further, it may be hers have altered by now."

Elizabeth did not think Jane so inconstant as that. Then, it had been some time, and it would have been foolish for Jane to keep pining. She'd no reason to think Mr. Bingley would ever return and renew their acquaintance. Without seeing Jane, Elizabeth realized she had no way to know, so she held her peace.

"I believe I have kept my side of our bargain," Mr. Darcy said, his tone mild.

"Indeed, sir, you have." Elizabeth pressed her lips together, trying to frame what she must say, for he had made an honest confession, and told her truths she hadn't necessarily cared for, as he'd implied he would. Again, Mr. Darcy had proven a man of his word.

"Then there is something you would care to say?" he prompted.

Elizabeth looked up at him, finding his eyes on her face. "I did not care for your behavior at the assembly the first night you were in

Hertfordshire."

He frowned, but she had the impression it was a thoughtful look, not censorious. Then he grimaced. "I was not behaving as I ought. I was aloof. It wasn't until I stopped to consider how my aunt's actions must seem to others that it occurred to me to wonder how mine are perceived. I do have an explanation, but it isn't justification."

"Then explain," she said, impressed he realized the difference between the two.

"Several of my friends in London invited me to a gathering the night before I left. They made me the focus of it, saying I wouldn't be in town again for some time. That rendered it impossible for me to leave early. In consequence, I was up and departing London just a few hours after going to bed. I wanted to sleep in the carriage, but Bingley's sisters insisted on talking to me." He grimaced, and Elizabeth couldn't help but sympathize.

"They also insisted on stopping at a tavern, which they claimed would take us only a few minutes," Mr. Darcy continued. "Between having trouble finding it and the inevitable delays in getting a meal, it cost us another four or five hours. When we arrived, I wanted to rest, but Bingley wanted to show us around Netherfield Park." Exasperation touched his tone. "I thought that at least I would get to bed at a reasonable time, but they all insisted we go to the assembly."

Mr. Darcy looked at her, his expression a bit sheepish. "In protest, I informed Bingley of my state and said that if he insisted I go, I would only do the bare minimum, dance with his sisters. It was rude of me, I realize, especially as no one there knew I was at the end of my tolerance. Looking back, I can see how it must have appeared to you, but please believe that is not how I meant it. It wasn't my intention to, in one night, offend the entirety of the community."

"Not the entire community," she allowed, smiling. "But of those you did offend, you managed to do so especially well with one in particular."

"I did?" He frowned. "It sounds like something I might do, but I can't recall how I could have. I did my best to keep myself, miserable company as I was that evening, away from everyone, to minimize my offensiveness. Who was it I especially insulted?"

"Me," she said.

His expression betrayed his shock. "You?"

"I believe Mr. Bingley did not take your declaration that you would dance with no one but his sisters seriously and attempted to persuade you otherwise. He may even have suggested you dance with someone? Someone in particular? Someone who was standing near enough to hear your reply."

Mr. Darcy halted midstride, taking Elizabeth off guard. She turned back to face him, clasping her hands before her.

"He suggested I dance with . . ." His voice trailed off. "I had forgotten." He closed his eyes for a moment, as if in pain. "I never meant . . . No, I spoke of honesty, and I did mean that. I wanted you to hear. I intended to be unkind. I was double annoyed that Bingley wouldn't leave me be and that he'd hit upon the one woman at the assembly who tempted me. I knew that if I danced with you, I must dance with all, or rumors would begin. I was angry, and lashed out at both the source of my temptation and my tormentor. You have my profound apology."

Had he just turned his insult into a compliment? As Mr. Darcy was not a skilled flatterer, she might even take his praise seriously. "It did get us off on the wrong foot," she allowed, smiling.

"I should have simply refused to go to the assembly. Once I went, I had an obligation to participate. I did not meet that obligation. The world doesn't adjust to de Bourghs or Darcys. I don't know why it has taken me so long to understand that."

She tried to read his expression, for his tone was strained, but he was looking away from her. Why didn't he want to meet her eyes?

"I fulfilled my social duties to my friends in London, to those riding in the carriage with me, at the tavern, and once we reached Netherfield Park," Mr. Darcy said.

"Then, when the people were beneath you, you treated them . . . rather, us . . . with contempt," Elizabeth said, understanding his embarrassment.

"I did. There is no excuse for it. I know it seems odd it took until today for me to realize I was wrong. It took watching you observe Lady Catherine's behavior for me to realize how ill-behaved I was." His expression became resolute as he finally met her gaze. "Miss Bennet, please forgive my behavior. I was boorish. When next I am in Hertfordshire, I will endeavor to make amends."

Everything she thought she knew about Mr. Darcy was disappearing like soap bubbles popping in the air. That didn't mean she was ready to marry him, but her animosity had dwindled from existence. "Though I cannot speak for all of Hertfordshire, I am willing to accept your apology, Mr. Darcy. What would you say to beginning our acquaintance over?"

"I would say, thank you." He offered his arm again.

Elizabeth took it. This time, they walked in a companionable way, their pace rambling. Elizabeth soon realized one thing she'd thought about Mr. Darcy was correct, he wasn't one to initiate a conversation. As she wanted to learn more about him, she would need to draw him out. "Did the tavern live up to expectations?"

His brow creased in confusion for a moment, smoothing as he smiled. "It did. They served a delicious meal. If I hadn't been so tired, I would have considered the detour reasonable. However, next time I go there, I think I'll plan to stay overnight."

While they walked, Elizabeth employed gentle prompting to engage Mr. Darcy in conversation. It wasn't as difficult as she'd first feared it would be, for he seemed eager to converse with her and they talked pleasantly for some time. When he talked about his home and his sister, she could tell he loved both. She'd never thought of Mr. Darcy as a man who could love a person or a place, but clearly he could, and deeply. She'd also never thought of him as a man of passion, but now understood that he was rather a person in which emotions ran deep, by far deep enough to generally keep below the surface.

Eventually, they found themselves on the path leading to the garden they'd met Miss de Bourgh and Colonel Fitzwilliam in earlier. After a slight hesitation, Mr. Darcy steered them down it. "We should likely check on them."

They rounded the last turn in the path to find Colonel Fitzwilliam and Miss de Bourgh now seated on the same bench. The colonel had his arm around her and their heads were close as they spoke in tones too low to hear. Mr. Darcy scuffed his foot, sending a stone clattering down the path. The couple on the bench started, Colonel Fitzwilliam standing. Elizabeth was surprised to see Miss de Bourgh blush.

"Darcy, Miss Bennet," Colonel Fitzwilliam said, nodding in greeting. He turned back to Miss de Bourgh, offering a hand, which she took as she came to stand at his side.

"May I assume you've accepted Richard's proposal?" Mr. Darcy asked Miss de Bourgh.

"Yes, I have," she said, still blushing. "I'm just a little nervous about telling my moth . . . That is, about telling Lady Catherine. I thought we could all go in together and face her." She turned to Elizabeth. "What about you, Miss Bennet? Have you decided to accept my cousin?"

Elizabeth hesitated, surprised to be placed in the position of answering in that moment. She realized that in the course of their walk, something had come together. From the first time she set eyes on him, Mr. Darcy had captured her attention, even when she didn't like him. In fact, though she'd been angry with him almost from the moment they met, she'd never been able to ignore him. He was forever in her thoughts. Somehow, with the reasons for her anger explained away, he still filled her mind. She realized a day without him would be an empty day indeed.

Turning to Mr. Darcy, she grinned up at him impishly. "Mr. Darcy is planning to take me to a certain out-of-the-way tavern for a very nice meal. I suppose it wouldn't be appropriate to accept were we not at least betrothed." She enjoyed watching his face as he understood her reference. She saw how well the expression of heartfelt delight became him.

A new set of footsteps on the path interrupted Miss de Bourgh's happy exclamation. Elizabeth, Darcy at her side, turned to see Mrs. Jenkinson walking hurriedly toward them. Far from her usual decorous self, she was wringing her hands.

"Mr. Kendall is here," Mrs. Jenkinson said. "He knew I planned to tell Lady Catherine today and was worried she would ask me to leave immediately, the dear man. He wanted to be here for me. Now she's asking him all sorts of questions. She claims to want to know what I'm getting into, but she's tormenting him. I was hoping you could deflect some of her attention. Will you come?"

"Yes, of course," Miss de Bourgh said. She started up the path. "Come, Richard."

Mr. Darcy made to follow, but Elizabeth put a hand on his arm, drawing him back. He turned to her, his look inquiring.

"There is just one more thing I need to know, before I can possibly permit you to declare our union to the world."

"What is it?" he asked, concern overshadowing his features. "Name it. Anything."

"Kiss me. I need to be sure we have passion, that--"

Apparently, Darcy didn't care what else she needed to be sure of, for his arms were about her. Elizabeth was sure they had passion the moment their lips touched, but he was doing too good a job proving it for her to want to interrupt.

"And do hurry," Mrs. Jenkinson's voice called, drifting back to them. "Lady Catherine insists it's going to rain."

Darcy either didn't hear her, or didn't care, for he only deepened their kiss.

Present Day, December, Pemberley . . .

Darcy took in his wife's smile, wondering what she was thinking about. It couldn't be their argument, for she wore a look of sublime happiness. Unless, of course, Elizabeth was so sure she was about to win that victory was invoking her smile.

He sighed, pushing away his hardly touched meal. If she was sure she was going to win, she wasn't far off the mark. At least, she was about to win the first part of the battle, for she was right. He'd learned long ago not to judge someone without knowing them. "I'll meet the boy."

She blinked, coming back from wherever her mind had taken her. "You will?"

"I will," he affirmed. Elizabeth's smile made the concession easy.

She jumped up from her chair. He noticed she hadn't eaten much either. She was halfway to the door before she stopped and turned back. "Well, come on," she said, gesturing for him to follow.

"To London, now?" he asked, standing even though he thought she was acting daft.

"No, to the front parlor."

Darcy frowned as he crossed the room. "Our front parlor?"

"I can't imagine barging into someone else's, especially at this time of day."

With mounting trepidation, Darcy followed her slender form from the breakfast parlor and through the house. "Why are we going to our front parlor?"

She didn't reply, merely increasing her stride.

When they neared the parlor, she slowed, smoothing her dress. She looked back at him, holding a finger to her lips to indicate silence, and started forward at a slow pace. Still frowning, Darcy followed.

They reached the open parlor door to find a fair-haired boy standing in the middle of the room. His back was to them and he was gazing up at the Christmas decorations. Elizabeth started forward, but Darcy put a staying hand on her shoulder, overwhelmed by how much the child resembled his father at that age, at least in form, height and locks.

Young George reached toward a delicate ornament surrounded by branches of evergreens, but didn't touch it. Instead, he dropped his hand, clasping both behind his back, and continued what appeared to be an examination of each piece. Even when his perusal brought him to a finely crafted miniature sailing ship and he leaned forward as if drawn closer by an unseen force, he didn't touch anything, which was nothing like Wickham.

Elizabeth reached up and placed her hand on top of Darcy's where it rested on her shoulder. He realized they'd been observing for several long minutes. He cleared his throat. The boy turned.

He looked like Wickham, and he didn't. His eyes . . . they were Bennet eyes. With a start, Darcy realized they were Elizabeth's eyes. Lydia Wickham hadn't had them, her father's eyes, but she'd passed on them to her son nonetheless. Those eyes were intelligent and, right now, worried.

"Hello George," Elizabeth said, her tone warm. "I would like you to meet your Uncle Darcy."

"Hello, sir," George said. He bowed. "I'm very pleased to meet you. Thank you for inviting me here while . . ." The boy's voice broke. He swallowed several times. "That is, Aunt Elizabeth said it may take a little while to discuss where it's best for me to go, now my mum is gone."

"You're welcome, George," Darcy said.

"I know it's an impo . . . imposition . . ." He screwed up his face in thought. "I know it's a bit of trouble, because it's nearly Christmas and everyone has a lot of things to do at Christmas, so we can't bother them. My mum always said so."

Darcy darted a surprised look at his wife, recalling that, for the first few years after Wickham died, she'd tried to get him to allow her sister and young George to visit for the holiday. He'd said no, always. He'd told her to send them money to visit other relatives, if need be, but that he wouldn't have Wickham's son in his home. Taking in the boys worried, respectful expression, Darcy realized that all those years ago, Anne had been right to call him a fool.

"Well, you're here now," Darcy said, offering a smile. "We were going to take a walk about the grounds today. Quite possibly, there will be snowballs, and a snowman. Would you like to come?"

"Really, sir?"

"Yes, really. A Darcy doesn't make an offer he doesn't intend to make good on. No man should." Darcy watched those intelligent Bennet eyes filing that information away.

"Then I should like that very much, sir. Thank you for inviting me."

"You are welcome, and you do not need to call me sir. You are my nephew. I would be pleased if you would call me Uncle Darcy."

"Thank you, Uncle Darcy."

"I'm happy you've come to spend Christmas with us, George," Elizabeth said, crossing to hug the boy.

Darcy took in his wife, a warm smile on her face and her arms about their nephew, the trimmings of the Yuletide surrounding them. He looked at the delicate sailing ship, an ornament his mother had given him as a child, and at the newly reupholstered chairs, that had seated generations of Darcys, set on either side of the fire.

Pemberley was his home. It was filled with the trappings of the Darcy family. It was also full of memories, both happy and sorrowful. Most of all, because of Elizabeth, it was filled with life and love. Darcy was not really a fool, and only a fool would turn the boy away.

~ The End ~

From Ashes to Heiresses

Prologue

Mr. Phillips sat down at his desk to write Mr. Gardiner.

My Dear Brother Edward,
It is with great sorrow I must inform you there was a fire at Longbourn. Most regretfully, it took place in the night and the entire family was abed. It can be considered a great act of fortune Jane and Elizabeth were not there, but the rest of the family perished.

Four servants escaped. Inquiries have led me to conclude the fire likely started in the parlor near the main staircase. It has come to light Lydia and Kitty were discovered experimenting with cigars near that area earlier in the evening. I would make no damning conclusions based on what little can be gleaned, but this may have started a fire that wasn't noticed until it raged out of control after everyone was settled for the night.

What I can say with moderate certainty is the servants' stairway was safe for longer than the main stairway. I may also report one of the servants who escaped heard Mrs. Bennet insisting she get her jewels. Sadly, those will be the last words any hear from our dear Mr. and Mrs. Bennet, Mary, Kitty or Lydia.

It is my understanding Jane and Elizabeth are with you in London, though planning to return soon. If this letter manages to reach you before they depart, please consider accompanying them. We will be on the lookout for them here as well. They will, of course, stay with us.

We have room for you and Mrs. Gardiner as well. I urge you to make whatever haste you can to join us here. I have a copy of Mr. Bennet's will, which names you and me as co-executors. Jane and Elizabeth will both be devastated. I believe your presence to be both necessary and helpful. The funerals will be held on Saturday.
Yours, etc.
J. Phillips

Chapter One

One Week Earlier...

Elizabeth was glad to be afforded a carriage, and a pleasant travel companion. She'd found her time in Kent interesting, to say the least, but was very eager to be reunited with Jane and to see her aunt and uncle Gardiner. She turned from the window, aware of Maria Lucas's excitement and wondering how long the girl could keep up her current level of decorum.

"Good gracious!" cried Maria, after a few minutes' silence, "it seems but a day or two since we first came! and yet how many things have happened!"

"A great many indeed," said her companion with a sigh.

"We have dined nine times at Rosings, besides drinking tea there twice! How much I shall have to tell!"

Elizabeth added privately, "And how much I shall have to conceal!"

Elizabeth was glad she had time for reflection during the journey to London, since she had much to think about. Mostly, she thought about Mr. Darcy and his abysmal proposal. Elizabeth had refused him angrily, accusing him of harming both his childhood friend, Mr. Wickham, and her sister, Jane. That very much seemed like the correct course of action at the time, especially since he'd added insult to her station and family to his already egregious crimes.

Now, when it was much too late, she realized she hadn't behaved as well as she should have. That didn't mean she wasn't still happy to have refused him. His proposal was nothing short of insulting.

He'd subsequently written her a letter, though, much to her surprise. In that letter, he explained the truth about Mr. Wickham. He also justified his conduct regarding Jane. While Elizabeth didn't agree with his motives for separating her most beloved sister and Mr. Bingley, she could see they weren't malicious. Mr. Darcy had acted as a friend must, making the deed nearly laudable. She was glad she would never see him again, because she was embarrassed, she'd misjudged him so completely and refused him with so little consideration for his emotions or for politeness.

Their journey was performed without much conversation, or any alarm; and within four hours of their leaving Hunsford they reached Mr. Gardiner's house, where they were to remain a few days with Elizabeth's aunt, uncle, cousins and Jane.

Jane looked well, and Elizabeth had little opportunity of studying her spirits, amidst the various engagements which the kindness of her aunt had reserved for them. But Jane was to go home with her, and at Longbourn there would be leisure enough for observation.

It was not without an effort, meanwhile, that she could wait even for Longbourn, before she told her sister of Mr. Darcy's proposals. To know that she had the power of revealing what would so exceedingly astonish Jane, and must, at the same time, so highly gratify whatever of her own vanity she had not yet been able to reason away, was such a temptation to openness as nothing could have conquered but the state of indecision in which she remained as to the extent of what she should communicate; and her fear, if she once entered on the subject, of being hurried into repeating something of Bingley which might only grieve her sister further.

For they had not all been mad. Mr. Bingley had indeed been on the verge of proposing to Jane, which would have given her a supreme happiness. Mr. Darcy's letter explained why he and Bingley's sisters persuaded Mr. Bingley not to do so. Mr. Darcy sharply objected to the behavior of Jane's and Elizabeth's younger sisters and parents. Though she still decried his interference, Elizabeth could see Mr. Darcy had some justification for his actions. It grieved her that the behavior of members of their family had taken such a disastrous toll on Jane's chance of happiness with the man she loved, and who appeared to love her.

Not enough, though, clearly. How could Mr. Bingley have loved Jane enough, after all, when he'd allowed himself to be persuaded away from her? As unhappy as losing him must make her sister, Elizabeth wasn't sure Jane should be with a man who could so easily remove himself.

***

When their visit with their aunt and uncle was over, Elizabeth and Jane left London amid a sea of well wishes and invitations to return. In truth, Elizabeth was a bit sad to depart. She loved her aunt and uncle, and her cousins, very much. She missed home, though, and she would be happy for a return to normality. Perhaps once in Longbourn again, she and Jane could both put their disastrous interactions with the opposite sex behind them.

The stage didn't offer the opportunity for private conversation, but it did give more chance for reflection than they'd known in the Gardiner's busy home. Elizabeth used some of that time for her own tumultuous thoughts and some for the study of Jane. Though her sister's emotions were hidden behind her usual appearance of serenity, Elizabeth was sure there was still an underlying sadness clinging to Jane. Her sister, it seemed, had not yet gotten over Mr. Bingley and his ill use.

When they disembarked in the town where the Bennets' carriage was supposed to meet them, Elizabeth was surprised to find it wasn't there. She'd written their father they would return today and received confirmation they would be met. It was only about six miles to Longbourn, sticking to the road, but they couldn't make the trip with their luggage.

"Do you think they have forgotten us?" she asked, turning to Jane.

"I daresay they're simply late. Let us wait a while and I am sure the carriage will arrive soon."

The three women went to the inn to wait. Maria Lucas was worried the carriage had lost a wheel. Jane calmed her fears and kindly engaged her in a discussion of what they would order at the inn. When the meal was eaten without the arrival of the carriage, Elizabeth inquired about hiring some conveyance to bring them home.

She soon located an inexpensive vehicle for hire. It was the only conveyance available within their means, but it didn't have enough room for all of them and their possessions. Not wanting to wait for another opportunity, she hired it regardless, telling the driver only Jane and Maria would need to ride.

Since Maria was becoming agitated at the wait, and since Lucas Lodge was no further than Longbourn, Elizabeth and Jane quickly decided to take Maria home first.

"I'll walk," Elizabeth said. "I've been inactive too long, and I'll enjoy it."

"Walk swiftly, then, or Lady Lucas will send out a carriage to find you," Jane said. She gave Elizabeth a smile and allowed the driver to hand her up.

It was a beautiful day for walking, made all the more delightful by the familiar scenery. When Elizabeth got close to Longbourn, she cut across a field, hungry for a glimpse of home after nearly two months' absence. She hurried up the final hill, knowing the house would be visible when she reached the crest. A smile on her face, she scanned the countryside before her.

Her searching gaze met with a smoldering ruin.

She broke into a run, her heart thrashing violently in her chest. When she got close, it was even worse than she'd thought. There was nothing left but the hearths. Wildly, she looked about, an anguished cry bubbling from her lips.

Where was everyone? Where was Jane? What had happened?

"Miss Bennet," a voice called.

Elizabeth turned to see a woman walking toward her, coming from the direction of one of the tenant cottages, a baby on her hip.

"Mrs. Smith," Elizabeth cried. With a shudder, she turned from the still smoking ruins and ran toward the woman. "What has happened?"

"There was a fire," Mrs. Smith said, unnecessarily. She shook her head, the movement slow and drenched in sorrow.

"Where is my family?"

"Dead."

"All of them?" Elizabeth asked in horror.

"Aye." Mrs. Smith drew in a long breath. She rocked the baby, though it didn't fuss, only watched Elizabeth with wide eyes. "Your parents are dead, and your younger sisters with them."

"Dead?" Elizabeth repeated. She took a step backward, dizziness assailing her.

"I'm sorry, miss."

Still looking at Elizabeth with wide eyes, the baby started to cry.

It was in a dazed blur Elizabeth, through the kindness of neighbors, eventually found herself at the Phillips. She walked up the steps and stood, unable to knock. Her mind filled with the image of her burned home. With such a fire and Mrs. Smith's word for it, she knew her family must be gone. Still, it seemed almost as if, were she not to enter and hear it from the respected figure of her uncle, it may not really be true.

The door opened, revealing the very man of her thoughts. "Elizabeth," Uncle Phillips said. "I was on my way to look for you. Jane is inside."

Elizabeth stared at him. She couldn't think of anything to say.

"Come in, dear," he said, stepping back and gesturing her into the hall.

Her movements stiff, Elizabeth stepped inside.

"You've heard, I take it?" her uncle asked in a quiet voice.

Elizabeth nodded. Tears built up in her eyes and she blinked, sending them streaming down her cheeks. "I saw the house," she said. Rather, those were the words she meant to say, but all that emerged were garbled sobs.

Her uncle put his arms about her, patting her on the back. Elizabeth gave in to her sorrow, weeping on his shoulder. It took her long moments to collect herself enough to relinquish her hold on him and allow him to lead her to Jane. Her only relief was that Jane had received the news at Lucas Lodge, not by the burnt-out shell that was once Longbourn.

***

The funerals took place that Saturday, the Gardiners arriving the day before. After their parents and sisters were laid to rest, Elizabeth and Jane sat down with their aunts and uncles in the Phillips parlor. Elizabeth knew they were there to discuss her and Jane's futures. She tried to muster the necessary interest, but her grief was too fresh for her to convince herself to care.

The only thing to penetrate the sorrow weighing on her was how wan Jane looked. Gentle soul that she was, Jane seemed to be even more distraught than Elizabeth. Elizabeth reached out and took her sister's hand. Squaring her shoulders, she resolved to attempt something better approaching normality, for Jane's sake.

Silence settled over the room, punctuated by the rustle of people fidgeting. Everyone looked about, avoiding each other's eyes. It was obvious no one knew where to begin.

"How are the servants?" Mr. Gardiner said, his tone gruff.

"Three of them have already found new employment," Mr. Phillips said. "The fourth, a maid, had already planned to marry a local farmer."

Mr. Gardiner nodded. Elizabeth realized she recalled hearing one of the maids was to wed. Mrs. Smith had named the servants who survived as well as those who hadn't. Elizabeth briefly regretted so little of her grief was for the servants who died. Her family's deaths were so overwhelming that the other deaths seemed inappropriately trivial. She resolved to include them in her prayers.

"As to the property, it is not our concern," Mr. Phillips said. "Since the estate was entailed, the heir will decide what to do about it."

Mrs. Gardiner leaned forward, clasping her hands before her. "Jane and Elizabeth should return with us to London. We have a room they can share."

"You have four children of your own to think of," Mrs. Phillips said, her tone sharp. "Consider the expense of two more mouths."

"The interest on the five thousand pounds their mother had should easily cover their expenses and give them an allowance."

Elizabeth squeezed Jane's hand, seeing tears form in her eyes at the mention of their mother.

Mr. Phillips cleared his throat. "There's something you should know about that money."

"If it isn't there, we will still take them in," Mr. Gardiner said. "We may have to cut a few corners, but we know our responsibility." He turned to look at Elizabeth and Jane. "And it will be our pleasure to have you."

Aunt Gardiner added a smiling nod to their uncle's words. "Of course, we will, and it truly would."

"No, we will take them in," Mrs. Phillips said. "Mr. Phillips and I have already decided."

"There are many advantages to living in London," Mrs. Gardiner said. "Jane and Elizabeth will flourish there."

Elizabeth wasn't certain that was true. She looked to Jane, but her sister's face was too wreathed in sorrow for Elizabeth to read her feelings on where they might live. She wished she'd thought to speak with Jane on the subject before now. Elizabeth might argue a side for them, but only if she knew what would better alleviate Jane's sorrow.

"They've had enough disruption in their lives. They should be surrounded by people they know," Mrs. Phillips countered.

"It would not be a disruption for Jane. She's spent months with us," Mrs. Gardiner said. "It will be good for them to get away from Hertfordshire and the sad memories here."

"If I may intervene," Mr. Phillips said. "I think what my wife is trying to express is your household will inevitably be centered around your young family. We will center ours around our nieces. We've never been blessed with children. I have no other living relatives. I've watched them grow up since they were infants, seeing them weekly. They are the daughters we never had. Please don't deprive us of them."

"We have to do what is best for them, not for us," Mrs. Gardiner said, looking more stubborn than Elizabeth had ever seen her.

"I can't argue with that, but I can disagree with what is best for them," Mr. Phillips countered.

The argument continued. Although the words remained polite, the voices were becoming strained. Elizabeth watched Jane carefully, gauging her level of distress. When it became too great, she decided she must try, at least, to make something happy of their circumstance. She leaned toward her sister, whispering, "At least they all want us. It would be awful if they were each arguing we should live with the other."

Jane managed a trembling smile, but tears stood out in her eyes. Elizabeth knew she must do something to stop the argument. Jane was becoming too upset and no progress toward a solution seemed to be forthcoming.

Were it up to Elizabeth alone, she would have chosen her London relatives, whom she preferred, though her Meryton ones had more space. Not knowing Jane's mind, though, and wanting to spare everyone's feelings, Elizabeth felt the solution was obvious. "We could spend half a year with each of you."

Mr. Gardiner and Mr. Phillips eyed each other. They looked to their wives. Mrs. Gardiner gave a miniscule nod. Mrs. Phillips looked rebellious but shrugged.

"I think that should be adjusted as needed," Mrs. Gardiner said. "It is too early to be thinking about suitors, but if someone is courting one of them, they should not be removed prematurely if it looks like a good connection."

"Yes," said Mrs. Phillips. She brightened. "Living in two locations will give them a better chance of meeting someone eligible. We all want that." She leaned across the table and patted Jane on the hand.

Elizabeth shook her head. She had no interest in courtship from any man. Her grief was still too new for her to struggle out from beneath the weight of it. There was no way she'd be able to manage the sort of amiability one should present to a suitor.

"Now, you were saying something about the money?" Mr. Gardiner asked Mr. Phillips, leaning back in his chair.

"Yes. Early on in their marriage, Mr. Bennet became concerned Mrs. Bennet was too extravagant. He didn't want to fight with her over money, but he was worried about it. He had to disclose his income, because of tithing, but his expenses, well, you know how expensive it is to run a farm." He looked about the table. "Well, no matter the details. The upshot is, he managed to put away around ten percent of his income almost every year without Mrs. Bennet knowing it."

Elizabeth raised her eyebrows. For a moment, surprise chased away grief. She'd no idea her father had such foresight, or was so cunning, or so economical.

"Mr. Phillips was doing the same with me," Mrs. Phillips said. The smile she gave her husband was indulgent. "I only found out about it two years ago."

"Two hundred pounds for more than twenty years," said Mr. Gardiner. "That comes to more than four thousand pounds."

"You forgot interest. It's closer to six thousand. Jane and Elizabeth will each have a bit more than five thousand pounds. Considering their situation, after their expenses and allowances are taken out, I believe the remainder of the money should be reinvested."

Elizabeth realized she was still staring at her Uncle Phillips and looked down. It was a great relief to know they were loved, and they wouldn't be a burden on those who cared for them. More than that, the money they would each have gave them a level of independence Elizabeth had never dared to hope for. She suppressed a sigh. The only bad thing was, without money to worry over, her mind had only the death of her parents and sisters to dwell on.

Chapter Two

Darcy listened to his sister, Georgiana, play the pianoforte with mixed feelings. She played beautifully and he enjoyed the music, but he suspected she played simply to avoid speaking with his guests. He'd already determined not to bring her out this coming season. She was still too shy. That her shyness extended to the Bingleys and the Hursts, whom she knew very well, served to emphasize the wisdom of Darcy's decision. How would Georgiana be able to cope with the numerous people she would have to meet during the season if she couldn't bring herself to interact with frequent companions?

On the score of Miss Bingley, Darcy concurred with his sister. Miss Bingley wasn't a comfortable guest. Her obvious attempts to attract him were very wearing. If Bingley weren't the most amiable of gentlemen, Darcy wouldn't routinely place himself within the same sphere as Bingley's sister.

Miss Bingley hadn't always been as trying. In truth, he hadn't noticed her behavior very much in the past. Her flattery had mirrored his typical lot and her pomposity had seemed reasonable. The change wasn't in Miss Bingley's behavior toward or around him, but more in himself.

Elizabeth Bennet had fully revealed her feelings for Darcy, and they had not been what he hoped, or even expected. Instead of admiring him as was his general due, especially from women in want of a husband, she'd criticized him. She'd gone so far as to accuse him of having a selfish disdain of the feelings of others. She'd labeled him a snob and elitist of the worst sort.

Looking about at the company he kept, Darcy was forced to consider the merit of her words. Miss Bingley, who sat watching Georgiana with obviously feigned delight, was trying to attract him and did everything she could to divide the world into people who were worth associating with and people who weren't. She looked down on the vast majority of people, as few fit her restricted criteria.

Her sister, Mrs. Hurst, wasn't quite as much of a sycophant as Miss Bingley, but she held just as many people in low esteem. That stood as proof of her snootiness, as she obviously valued social standing more than personal merit. Mrs. Hurst's husband was of unquestionably good lineage, but held only a modest estate, with an income of about half of what Mr. Bennet had. Mr. Hurst lived for his meals, naps, and cards.

Darcy had always tolerated Miss Bingley and the Hursts because of his friendship with Bingley and because they were the people he was expected to associate with. They were of the correct social class, age and lineages, though there was the shadow of trade in the Bingleys' past. Were those criteria truly the best way to establish with whom to fill one's days?

Darcy looked about the room again. Miss Bingley, seeing his gaze on her, stifled a yawn and gave him a fawning smile. Mrs. Hurst was playing with her bracelets, not even pretending to enjoy Georgiana's performance. Mr. Hurst was asleep on the sofa.

Maybe Georgiana had a point. Maybe Darcy should find a way to avoid talking to most of his guests. The more he considered his reasons for the company he kept, the less substantial they seemed. Instead, why not surround himself with people whose company he actually cared for, regardless of their station?

Darcy glanced over his shoulder at Bingley, wondering if he would be up for a game of billiards. Bingley was seated at a desk, going through the post. At least he wasn't pretending to pay attention, though he was sure to get an earful from his sisters later for not making the effort. Darcy would be daft not to realize they had ideas about Bingley wedding Georgiana. In spite of Bingley's imperfect lineage, Darcy would have welcomed the match, were there any sign of romantic affection between them. Even before Elizabeth's criticism of him had awakened him to some of his less savory characteristics, Darcy knew it would be better for his sister to have a man as good hearted and financially sound as Bingley than one with a title.

"Oh, no," Bingley exclaimed.

"What is the matter?" Darcy asked, turning more fully around in his seat.

Georgiana's fingers stilled on the keys.

"Sir William Lucas wrote me. Longbourn has burned down. The family died."

Darcy's heart froze in his chest. Elizabeth, dead?

"Poor Miss Bennet," Miss Bingley said. "She was very lovely."

"She wasn't home," Bingley said, his eyes fixed on the words he was reading.

The relief in Bingley's voice spoke volumes, his expression shifting from horrified to merely troubled. Darcy was peripherally aware of Bingley's sisters exchanging looks. He watched Bingley read on, too shocked by the loss of Elizabeth to speak.

"Neither was her sister Elizabeth," Bingley said.

Logically, Darcy knew it had been mere seconds between revelations, but an eternity of time drew to a close at Bingley's words. Darcy found himself able to breathe again, his heart shuddering back to life. He realized there was pain in his hands and looked down, finding them tightly fisted. Slowly, he uncurled his fingers.

"The Miss Elizabeth Bennet you wrote to me of?" Georgiana asked from her seat at the piano.

Glancing at his sister, Darcy also took in Miss Bingley's narrowed eyes and the flash of loathing there. "Yes, that Miss Elizabeth." Darcy turned back to Bingley. "You mean to say Mr. and Mrs. Bennet are gone, along with the home and three younger sisters?"

"Yes. Miss Bennet and Miss Elizabeth were safely away. Sir William says they'd been in London, Miss Bennet for some time." Bingley glanced at Miss Bingley. "I'm surprised she didn't call on you when she was in London."

"She did," Mr. Hurst said, surprising Darcy, who hadn't realized he was awake. "Sometime in January, I think. Your sisters returned the call a month later."

Everyone looked at him.

Bingley surged to his feet, swiveling to face Miss Bingley. "Why didn't you tell me?"

"Because I thought it wouldn't be good for you to see her," Miss Bingley said. "Louisa and I thought you were too likely to fall under her spell again."

"What else does the letter say?" Darcy asked, wanting to avoid further discussion of Miss Bennet's visit to London. He'd known she was there and had gone along with Miss Bingley's decision not to inform Bingley.

Bingley looked down. "Miss Bennet and Miss Elizabeth will be spending their summers in Meryton with the Phillips and their winters in London with the Gardiners."

"Transferred from household to household," Miss Bingley said. "That's what happens to poor, unwanted relatives, and they are going between a country attorney and a man in trade."

Bingley lifted an angry visage. "The behavior of their relatives does not make them less worthy or less kind."

"True," Darcy said, eliciting several startled looks.

Bingley sat abruptly, reaching for a clean page. "I must write her and offer my condolences."

No one asked who Bingley meant by *her*.

"You can't write her," Miss Bingley cried.

Bingley paused in the act of preparing writing supplies. He frowned, turning to Darcy.

"You really can't," Darcy said. "You can write Mr. and Mrs. Phillips and offer them your condolences."

"Yes. That's what you should do," Miss Bingley said. She cast Darcy a smile.

Bingley was still frowning, a deep line marking his brow. He shook his head. "I'm going to do more than that. I'm going there." He stood once more.

"Charles, no," Mrs. Hurst exclaimed, but Bingley left the room.

Darcy was torn between the foolishness of Bingley returning to Hertfordshire and a longing to accompany him. Surely, Bingley knew to return now would be tantamount to a proposal to Miss Bennet? Or would it be? He leased a house there and should be able to come and go as he pleased. There would be speculation, but that should not matter. Did Bingley care about that? Considering the look of terror on Bingley's face when he took in the first words of the letter, maybe he didn't mind the speculation that he might marry Miss Bennet, because he planned to do so.

Leaving the piano, Georgiana came over to sit beside Darcy.

"Mr. Hurst, do something," Mrs. Hurst cried.

"I am doing something." Mr. Hurst settled back onto the sofa. "I'm taking a nap."

"Louisa, we can't permit him to go," Miss Bingley said. "You know how he is. It was all we could do to keep him from proposing to that low woman before. Imagine now, when she's in distress? There will be no stopping him."

Georgiana touched Darcy's sleeve. "Since this is the same Miss Elizabeth you wrote me about last autumn, perhaps you should go with Mr. Bingley," she said in a soft voice. "It must have been awful for her to lose her family and home."

"That's a good idea," he said, standing.

"What?" Miss Bingley said. "You too, Mr. Darcy? What is this draw Hertfordshire has?"

Darcy could tell by the venomous undertones in her voice she suspected what the allure of Hertfordshire was, and did not condone it. He bowed to the room. "I beg your leave."

"Mr. Darcy, at least assure us that you go there to prevent Charles from doing anything foolish," Mrs. Hurst said.

"I can assure you of that, madam." There was no reason to elaborate on the fact he was growing more and more certain the only foolish thing Bingley could do would be not to propose to Miss Bennet. "Georgiana," he added with another bow, returning his sister's smiled.

As he strode from the room, Darcy assured himself that him being there wouldn't be in any way a public declaration of affection. People would assume he was there to support Bingley, as he would, in whatever choice Bingley made. Unless Elizabeth had revealed his proposal, something he did not think she would do, no one had reason to suspect his true motives were much more convoluted.

He must assure himself Elizabeth was being well provided for and, at the same time, attempt to understand his inability to put her from his thoughts, in spite of her adamant and thorough rejection. Maybe seeing her again would rid him of the demon that was his affection for her.

Or maybe seeing him again, changed as he was by her words, would soften her regard. He preferred that scenario. Smiling, Darcy strode through Pemberley, making ready to travel.

Chapter Three

It took Elizabeth little time to realize no amount of financial hardship would have distracted from the harsh reality of her family's death. Everything they did seemed to center around death. They made black dresses. They endured seemingly endless condolence calls and received piles of well-intentioned letters.

Elizabeth answered the letters as politely as she could. She took on the bulk of that task as Jane kept crying and smearing the ink. Jane did her best with the callers, sitting beside Elizabeth in bereaved silence while uncomfortable people spoke platitudes. Most people were very kind to them, which did help to buoy Elizabeth's spirits. Many more came than she would have expected, like Colonel Forster, commander of the local militia, who was very polite and thoughtful.

Another unexpected, and to Elizabeth's mind unwanted, caller was Lieutenant Wickham. He entered with a too-low bow and a charming smile. Elizabeth wondered how she could ever have considered his smug and ingratiating countenance pleasing.

"What lovely ladies," he said. "I didn't know black could make someone so attractive."

He included her Aunt Phillips in his sweeping glance, but his gaze came to rest on Jane, where it lingered overlong. Elizabeth found that odd, as he'd never paid Jane much attention before. Jane met his regard with a tentative smile.

In that moment, Elizabeth wished she'd made the time to enlighten Jane on the truth of Mr. Wickham's character while they'd been in London with the Gardiners. Not that there hadn't been time since returning, but her mind had been too occupied with the loss of their family to think about Mr. Wickham and Mr. Darcy.

"I've come to add my deepest sympathies to the well wishes I'm sure you've already garnered," Mr. Wickham said. "To lose your family, and you both still so young, is a tragedy indeed."

"Thank you," Jane murmured.

"I realize you, in particular, Miss Bennet, are of a very sensitive nature," he continued. "I know this time must be very trying for you indeed."

Jane looked to Elizabeth, her brow creased, before turning back to Mr. Wickham. "Elizabeth and I are both quite distraught."

"Yes, but your sister must admit you are the more sensitive. You may think I hadn't noticed, but how could I not?"

Jane looked to her again.

Elizabeth frowned. "It is true, Mr. Wickham. Jane's sensitive nature is legendary, which is why we must not distress her by speaking of it, or by allowing any visitors to stay over long."

"I agree with you on the first count, Miss Elizabeth." Mr. Wickham didn't look at her, but kept his smile aimed at Jane. "I beg your pardon for disagreeing on the second, however. I think the distraction of company is what Miss Bennet wants. Distraction and, dare I suggest, a walk?"

"Certainly," Jane said the same time as Elizabeth said, "No, thank you," in overly strident tones.

Jane turned a sad smile on Elizabeth. "I would like to get out, but I don't wish to inconvenience you, Lizzy. I'm sure Mr. Wickham will keep me respectful company."

Elizabeth wished more than ever she'd told Jane Mr. Wickham was no longer in her favor. "If you wish to walk, I shall accompany you."

"No, I wouldn't think of imposing on you," Jane said. "I'd rather not go out than do so."

"Surely you would not deprive your sister of some respite from her grief?" Mr. Wickham said.

"No, I would not," Elizabeth replied, trying not to glare at him. She no longer trusted him as she might once have. "Do go on, Jane. I'm content to remain here. Stay on the streets, though, won't you. We don't have a maid to send along."

She gave them both a smile, settling back in her seat. She did want Jane to get out. It had been weeks since their return. There was no reason her sister should sit there mourning at all moments of the day. If allowing Jane to walk with Mr. Wickham was what it took to see her happy, then Elizabeth would allow it, but she wouldn't let Jane go unchaperoned. She would make a reason to go after them.

"Miss Elizabeth, Mrs. Phillips," Mr. Wickham said, bowing.

Jane stood and he offered his arm, increasing Elizabeth's unease. She kept her smile in place until they left the room.

"Oh, what a handsome young man Mr. Wickham is," Mrs. Phillips said. "Only, I thought he was a friend of yours, Elizabeth. Why should he ask Jane to walk?"

"You know, Aunt Phillips, I should like to find out," Elizabeth said, standing. "I think I shall join them after all. It may be I can tease his reasons from him."

"I daresay teasing is at the heart of it, Elizabeth. You didn't show yourself pleased enough to see him, as you ought to have, so he is teasing you by paying attention to Jane. Don't let that go on too long, dear, or he'll take a liking to her. There's no man could resist taking a liking to our Jane, given half a chance."

"I'm sure you're right," Elizabeth said. Hurrying from the room, she fetched her bonnet and went outside. She could see Jane farther down the street, on Mr. Wickham's arm. Pressing her lips into a firm line, Elizabeth strode after them.

She didn't join them, but rather trailed behind. She truly didn't wish to ruin any slight enjoyment Jane could contrive from the day. She simply couldn't bring herself to trust Mr. Wickham, though. There was something unsettling in the way he was lavishing attention on Jane.

The day was warm enough, but it was windy and fluffy clouds sailed through the sky high above. Elizabeth followed them down the street and up the lane, worried when it appeared they were leaving town. Once free of Meryton, they paused beside a little used path. Elizabeth could see Jane shake her head, dropping his arm. Mr. Wickham leaned close, speaking animatedly. Jane hesitated a moment, then nodded. He offered his arm again and Jane hesitantly took it.

As they started up the path, Elizabeth lengthened her strides, closing the distance between them and keeping Jane in sight. She was doubly concerned now. There was no reason for Mr. Wickham to persuade Jane to go meandering through such a relatively uninhabited area. Not one Elizabeth would approve of, leastwise.

She drew closer but still didn't join them. In the time it took her to shorten the distance, restraint had somewhat reasserted itself. Jane was perfectly intelligent and very proper. If she'd agreed with whatever Mr. Wickham had said to her, it was likely acceptable. There was no reason for Elizabeth to barge in on their walk and make a hash of things.

A cottage drew into view, the reason for the path, though Elizabeth knew it had been abandoned the past summer. It stood atop a hill on a bit of cleared land and Elizabeth hung back farther. She didn't want them to turn to appreciate the view, likely why they'd come, and spot her.

Elizabeth moved behind some tall bushes, peeking out from the obscuring brush. She was feeling more and more like the worst sort of voyeur and a terrible sister. She pursed her lips, wondering if she should return to the Phillips. After all, Jane and Mr. Wickham must return the way they'd come, and what explanation would she have when they spotted her ahead of them on the way back?

As they crested the hill, Mr. Wickham dropped to the ground. Elizabeth went still in surprise, wondering what had befallen him. Jane came to her knees beside him. Elizabeth could see them speaking animatedly and hear their worried tones, but she couldn't make out the words. Jane stood. With what seemed like effort on both parts, Jane helped Mr. Wickham to his feet. He pointed toward the cottage. Jane ducked under his arm, helping him toward it.

Worried for both Jane and Mr. Wickham, Elizabeth untangled her skirts from the brush she hid in. Returning to the trail, she hurried up the remaining distance to the cottage. Reaching it, she was surprised to find the door closed. Tentatively, she pushed against it, but it didn't budge, appearing to be bolted.

Suddenly weary again, Elizabeth didn't knock. She backed away, looking about the clearing to no avail. With hurried steps, she circled the cottage, stopping when she found a window. It was shuttered, but several of the slats were missing. Ducking slightly, she peered in.

The cottage was filled with more light than she would have expected, mainly coming from a hole in the roof. Still, it took Elizabeth a moment to sort out their forms in the gloomy interior. When she did, she found Mr. Wickham with his back to the door. Jane stood across the room from him. Though in profile, Elizabeth could see the startled look on her face.

"...the door?" Jane was saying.

"So we may go undisturbed, my love," Mr. Wickham said.

Elizabeth gasped, smothering the sound with her hand.

"Your... I beg your pardon?" Jane said.

"Miss Bennet, you must allow me to tell you how ardently I admire and love you."

"What?"

"I had to get you alone." Mr. Wickham walked toward her. "The regiment will be leaving in a few days. I missed you all winter. I thought my case was hopeless, because you were taken in by Mr. Bingley."

"Taken in?" Jane stared at him, obviously dumfounded.

"Yes. He never cared for you as I do. Why would he leave you if he truly loved you? I, however, have remained."

"He...he may come back. He said he would come back."

Mr. Wickham was quite near Jane now. Elizabeth wanted to tell her to run, but where would Jane run to? Jane stared at him as he moved closer and closer. Reaching out, he grabbed for her.

Jane tried to duck away, but he was quicker. He pulled her to him, pressing his lips to hers. She thrashed, wrenching her head away and flailing at him ineffectually. Elizabeth cried out, yanking on the shutters.

Mr. Wickham stopped moving, looking about. Elizabeth went still. He peered toward the window.

Jane pulled free. "Mr. Wickham. What are you doing? This is not appropriate." She angled around him, moving toward the door.

Mr. Wickham turned back to Jane. "You are compromised. You have no choice but to marry me. You don't know how happy—"

"She certainly is not," Elizabeth cried through the window.

Mr. Wickham whirled, looking startled. Behind him, Jane crept toward the door.

"I've been here all along," Elizabeth said, striving to make enough commotion so Mr. Wickham wouldn't realize Jane was escaping his grasp. "I saw everything. You should be ashamed of yourself, Mr. Wickham."

"She has to marry me. After word of this gets out, no one else will have her," Mr. Wickham said.

"She's better off never marrying than wedding you," Elizabeth said.

Jane reached the door. Mr. Wickham turned as she pulled the latch open, but she flung the door wide and rushed out. Abandoning her post at the window, Elizabeth ran back around the house. She found Mr. Wickham on his knees before Jane, holding one of her hands, though she was obviously trying to pull away.

"Jane," he said.

"She is not Jane to you," Elizabeth snapped, hurrying to Jane's side.

"Miss Bennet," Mr. Wickham continued, shooting Elizabeth a scowl. "You must know how beautiful you are and how you can drive a man to distraction. That is what happened just now, but I will do right by you. I love you. Marry me."

Jane wrenched her hand away.

Elizabeth caught a glimpse of how red it was before Jane cradled it against her chest.

Jane drew her shoulders back, raising her chin. "I would rather remain alone than be coerced into marrying you."

"You may have to test that. You know I'm right. No one else will take you now."

Jane glared at him.

Mr. Wickham stood. He shrugged, dusting off his uniform. "Have it your way. Once you realize I've spoken the truth, you'll come begging me to take you."

Elizabeth and Jane trained matching looks of disdain on him. He gave them a jaunty smile before turning and walking away. Just before he disappeared into the woods, he looked back and waved.

Long moments passed while they waited, making sure he was gone. Elizabeth heard a ragged inhalation and looked over to see Jane on the verge of tears. Turning, she took Jane into her arms. Elizabeth made no attempt to stop her from crying, even though Jane sobbed the entire walk back to Meryton. Anyone seeing them would attribute Jane's tears to understandable grief.

Chapter Four

Darcy and Bingley called upon Mr. Phillips the same day they arrived in Hertfordshire. They were shown into a small parlor. Looking about, Darcy could see the contents of the room were not new, but were well cared for and in decent, though outdated, taste. All and all, it was a nicer room than he would have credited the Phillips and rather pleasant.

It would have been made exceedingly pleasant had it contained Elizabeth and Miss Bennet, but they were absent. Darcy settled into a chair, aware it wouldn't be in good form to ask about their whereabouts. Bingley, his gaze searching the room in an obvious manner, slowly sat as well.

"Mr. Darcy, Mr. Bingley," Mr. Phillips said. "This is a pleasant surprise, though quite unexpected. Have you decided to return to Netherfield Park, Mr. Bingley?"

"I should like to." Bingley leaned forward in his chair. "That is, I mean to, depending…Rather, we shall see." He looked to Darcy for help.

"We've come to express our condolences," Darcy supplied.

"All this way? That is exceedingly generous of you." Mr. Phillips studied them for a moment. "I am remiss in not offering you refreshments."

"That isn't necessary," Darcy said.

"I should have thought to offer immediately, of course. I do tend to forget these things when my wife isn't about to remind me. Mrs. Phillips is currently at Lucas Lodge." He smiled slightly. "Jane and Elizabeth have taken a walk. They've been gone some time. Are you sure you wouldn't care for something?"

Bingley gave him a pleading look. Darcy was tempted to take Mr. Phillips up on his offer to allow them to remain until Elizabeth and Miss Bennet returned. After this call, their condolences having been offered, they would have no ready excuse to return.

"Uncle," Elizabeth said, bursting into the room.

Darcy turned to her, astounded anew by the uncommon loveliness of her face. How he couldn't have noticed it on their initial meeting, he didn't know. She was especially lovely in that moment, her eyes flashing and face flushed.

"Pardon me," Elizabeth said, looking about the room. Her eyes met his questioningly. "I did not realize we had guests."

"Miss Elizabeth," Darcy said, standing to bow.

Mr. Phillips and Bingley stood as well, offering their greetings.

"Mr. Darcy." Elizabeth dropped a curtsy.

"Miss Bennet," Bingley said bowing a second time.

Darcy could see Bingley was looking past Elizabeth. For the first time, he realized her sister hovered behind her. Miss Bennet was rapidly wiping her eyes and cheeks. He gathered she'd been crying. When he turned back to Elizabeth, Darcy realized anger flashed in her eyes. Could she be that displeased to see him? Or was Bingley the focus of her ire? She'd made no secret of thinking he'd broken her sister's heart.

"Uncle," Elizabeth reiterated. She reached back, taking Miss Bennet's arm and tugging her into the room.

Darcy frowned. Something was not right in the image of the two young ladies before him. Miss Bennet seemed almost afraid, and now that Elizabeth was casting off her surprise at seeing them, her anger was a palpable thing. Darcy couldn't bring himself to think anyone in the room was deserving of that much animosity, even him.

"What's wrong, my dear?" Mr. Phillips came forward to take Miss Bennet's hands.

"What is wrong is that Mr. Wickham attempted to compromise Jane." Elizabeth's voice was fierce. She wrapped an arm about Miss Bennet's shoulder.

"He did what?" Bingley exclaimed. He looked about as if seeking the man.

"He tricked her into taking an unused path," Elizabeth said.

"He told me Lydia had spoken to him of a place she loved to go, where she'd secreted some small sentimental objects she adored. He said he wanted to help me find them so we could have something to remember her by," Miss Bennet said, her voice breaking as tears overwhelmed her once more.

"He lured Jane into the Evans' abandoned cottage and locked the door," Elizabeth said. "Not trusting him, I was following them. When the door wouldn't open, I went round to a window. He grabbed her and forced his attentions on her."

"He did what?" Bingley repeated, looking stunned.

"He only kissed me," Miss Bennet said, her face turning red. "It was awful."

"He kissed you and demanded you marry him." Elizabeth was clearly livid.

Darcy reflected Wickham was fortunate Miss Elizabeth wasn't a man. Elsewise, Wickham would be forced to meet her at dawn. Darcy was sorely tempted to call his onetime playmate out himself. Coercing women was a new low for Wickham.

"He's a kidnapper," Bingley said.

"I doubt a court would see it that way," Mr. Phillips said, shaking his head.

"I'll challenge him to a duel," Bingley said.

Darcy could see his friend's astonishment was shifting into anger. "If you are trying to preserve Miss Bennet's reputation, that won't help." Darcy watched Bingley comprehend the situation. A duel fought over a woman, especially by a man who was not a relative, would seriously damage her reputation.

"Dueling is illegal," Mr. Phillips said with a sigh. "Yes, I've been wishing I were twenty years younger and was adept with both sword and pistol for the last few minutes, but it would accomplish nothing."

"If I may be so insensitive as to ask, why does Mr. Wickham want to marry Miss Bennet?" Darcy asked. "I thought Mr. Bennet had little to leave and am familiar with what Wickham seeks in a spouse."

"There is a rumor going around that the Miss Bennets are heiresses."

Something about the closed look on Mr. Phillips' face and his tone made Darcy wonder how much truth there was to the rumor. Could Mr. Bennet have been a better businessman than Darcy surmised?

"Mr. Wickham nearly succeeded in marrying an heiress, Miss Mary King, a month ago," Mr. Phillips continued. "Her uncle took her away."

"He said he's always loved me," Miss Bennet said. "He claimed he never said anything before because he knew he couldn't compete wi--" She broke off, her tear-filled eyes going to Bingley.

"I don't find it a stretch to believe a man could be driven to distraction by Miss Bennet's beauty," Bingley said.

Darcy raised his eyebrows. A glance showed him similar expressions on Elizabeth's and Mr. Phillips' faces. Bingley and Miss Bennet looked at each other, seemingly unaware of anyone else.

Elizabeth turned to Darcy. "As little as I think of Mr. Wickham's character, this seems a rash action even for him."

"Mr. Wickham likely has debts," Darcy said.

"He does," Mr. Phillips said. When they turned to him, he shrugged. "An attorney hears things others don't. I've told two of my clients they should take action against him before his unit leaves or lose their money. Neither want to do so, because he is popular. Now, I wonder if I should stop pressing them. If he faced debtors' prison and knew the source, the first thing he would do would be to malign Jane. Though I admit, it would give me satisfaction to see the man locked away, and if he didn't learn the source, it may be the best protection for her."

Darcy frowned. He wouldn't mind seeing Wickham locked away either, but he doubted it would come to that. Instead, Wickham would attempt to blackmail Darcy into paying his debts again by threatening to expose Georgiana's near elopement with him. Darcy caught Elizabeth's eyes on him and wondered if her thoughts traversed a similar path.

"Locked away?" Miss Bennet repeated. She'd dried her tears again and looked steadier by far than when she and Elizabeth had arrived. "I shouldn't wish to be responsible for anyone going to prison. I wouldn't be able to live with knowing I'd caused anyone such suffering, even Mr. Wickham."

"But he attempted to force you into marriage." Bingley's tone evidenced anger once more. "He deserves prison or worse."

"I still don't want it to be done over me."

"He wouldn't go to debtors' prison because of you, dear," Mr. Phillips said. "He would go because of his debts. It is, after all, where he belongs by dint of his behavior. We must do something to prevent him from slandering your reputation and ruining your prospects."

Taking in the way Bingley looked at Miss Bennet, Darcy didn't think she needed to fear for her marriage prospects. Miss Bennet didn't know that, however. She turned a pleading look on her sister.

"Though we cannot control the actions of everyone in the community, I ask that none of you consider putting Mr. Wickham in debtor's prison," Elizabeth said in a firm tone. "I have no wish for my sister to allot any of her kind spirit to worrying over Mr. Wickham. Causing Jane more misery will not alleviate the upset he's produced and will instead only place more unhappiness on her shoulders."

Miss Bennet cast Elizabeth a grateful smile.

Darcy gave a nod of his head to indicate his understanding. "Would you mind if we threaten Mr. Wickham with debtors' prison?" Darcy thought Miss Bennet too tender hearted, but she wouldn't be a fitting match for Bingley if she weren't. As he could observe how much Bingley cared for her, he must be pleased by her gentle nature instead of regretting it.

"What do you have in mind?" Elizabeth asked.

"Can anyone speculate on the next time Mr. Wickham will be in public?" Darcy asked.

"Tonight, at Lucas Lodge," Mr. Phillips said. "Sir William is throwing a party for the officers. We are invited, but I'd thought not to attend, considering."

"I should like to attend," Bingley said. "I have a thing or two to say to Mr. Wickham. But I don't believe we were invited."

"No one knows you are in town," Elizabeth said. "I am sure Sir William would never turn you away, however."

Darcy nodded, acknowledging the likely truth of her statement. "Knowing Wickham as I do, I think I can say with surety he will attend the event. He will not miss a chance to be charming and partake of food and drink provided by another, and he will not fear meeting either of you because you are still in mourning. I propose we all attend Sir William's event. I have a plan which I think shall satisfy everyone, but it requires us all to participate."

"Then let us hear it," Mr. Phillips said.

All eyes turned to Darcy. He proceeded to elaborate on his plan. It pleased him to see how quickly both Elizabeth and her uncle registered understanding, and then satisfaction.

They spent nearly an hour discussing the details. In spite of the seriousness of the situation, Darcy thoroughly enjoyed himself. He knew his pleasure in the conversation stemmed in small part from contemplating Wickham's takedown and in great part from Elizabeth. Darcy hadn't enjoyed himself so much in quite some time. Not, in fact, since the last time he'd sparred with her.

Miss Bennet was timid at first, clearly still recovering from what had happened, and Darcy worried they wouldn't be able to carry off the plan. At Elizabeth's suggestion, they rehearsed their scenario several times, with her playing the part of Wickham. Darcy could tell each rendition increased Miss Bennet's confidence.

Mrs. Phillips returned, and Mr. Phillips explained everything to her, even giving her a role to play. She had trouble taking in both what had happened and the plot they'd hatched. After some time, however, Mr.

Phillips' repeated explanations and a great deal of patience got Mrs. Phillips into the spirit of the thing.

At first, the need for the careful reconstruction of Mrs. Phillips' beliefs about Wickham tried Darcy's patience, though he was careful not to show it. As the conversation went on, he found himself contrasting Mr. Phillips' behavior toward his wife with Mr. Bennet's toward Mrs. Bennet. Darcy would never say anything to Elizabeth, but he thought Mr. Phillips was a better husband for an unintelligent woman than Mr. Bennet had been.

Darcy stood slightly to the side, watching Elizabeth take Miss Bennet and Mrs. Phillips through their final repetition of the plan. If Darcy had his way, he would never need to know what sort of husband he would make in similar circumstances. He would have Elizabeth, whose quick wit and clever tongue outshone even her lovely smile.

Chapter Five

Elizabeth followed Jane to their room to make ready for the evening. Now that she and Jane were alone, she was aware of sorrow threatening to overwhelm her once more. Almost angry at the emotion, she tamped it down as best she could. There was no way to lessen her heartbreak over losing her parents, sisters and home, but she knew she must be strong now for Jane. She fervently hoped Jane could be strong too. They had to get Mr. Wickham out of their lives and make sure he stayed out.

Mr. Darcy and Mr. Bingley had returned to Netherfield Park to make their preparations as well. As Elizabeth changed her dress and arranged her hair, she found contemplating Mr. Darcy's behavior a surprisingly effective distraction from her grief. She'd never seen him so relaxed and comfortable. He'd treated her Uncle Phillips with respect. No, Mr. Darcy had treated her uncle as an equal. On top of that, he hadn't shown the slightest bit of annoyance at either her aunt's slowness in learning her part or for Jane's timidity. It was a welcome change, for she couldn't have borne an afternoon with a haughty Mr. Darcy. Not with her nerves already stretched thin by mourning. Elizabeth thought kindness suited his eyes.

Later that evening as they trailed their aunt and uncle into Lucas Lodge, Elizabeth could see Jane's nervousness return. Jane stopped in the entry hall, for she was to wait above stairs in the youngest Lucas's room. He was a boy of about seven and adored Jane. Elizabeth knew he would ask her to read to him or play soldiers. She hoped it would keep Jane distracted until their aunt fetched her.

"It will all go just as we've planned," Elizabeth whispered.

"How can you be so certain?" Jane asked.

"Mr. Darcy knows Mr. Wickham quite well. They grew up together. Don't worry."

Jane managed a weak smile. "I feel awkward being here while we're still in deep mourning. People will think we didn't love Mama, Papa and our sisters enough." Jane was on the verge of tears.

"People will come to understand. Please don't fret. We'll have this behind us soon."

Jane nodded, looking unconvinced.

Elizabeth gave her a quick hug, then a gentle shove toward the steps. After watching Jane go up, she hurried after her aunt and uncle. She reached them in time to accept the arm her uncle offered.

Entering the large parlor on her uncle's arm, Elizabeth searched through the sea of familiar faces for Mr. Wickham. It didn't take long to spot him standing beside the refreshment table speaking with Colonel Forster. Elizabeth was grimly pleased. Wickham's choice of both location and companion couldn't be better.

"He's by the refreshment table," Elizabeth said under her breath to her uncle.

He nodded, adjusting their course.

As they crossed the room, Elizabeth tried to ignore the stunned looks. She hoped what she'd assured Jane was true; people would understand the need for their presence in Lucas Lodge tonight and not condemn them for being out so soon. She tilted up her chin, pressing her lips into a firm line. Grief laden as she was, she couldn't muster a smile.

Elizabeth knew the moment Colonel Forster saw her, for surprise suffused his face. Mr. Wickham spun around, likely in response to the startled look Colonel Forster was giving her. Elizabeth squared her shoulders, meeting his gaze.

"Mr. Wickham, how dare you force your attentions on my niece," her Uncle Phillips roared.

Eyes turned toward them. Nearby conversations trailed off, only to resurface as startled whispers.

"I did no such thing," Mr. Wickham said.

Elizabeth watched him look at her speculatively. It was their plan he assume she was there as a substitute victim, Jane being too gentle for confrontation. Without Jane delivering it, the charge carried much less weight. They didn't wish Mr. Wickham to feel too threatened until their trap closed around him and it was too late.

"Furthermore, I should call you out for such an accusation," Mr. Wickham said.

Elizabeth did her best not to grimace at his poorly feigned outrage.

"Dueling is illegal and challenging a man who is a quarter of a century older than you and who has never fenced and never fired a pistol is an act of cowardice," her Uncle Phillips said contemptuously.

"You call me a coward and yet refuse to consider a way of proving I'm not?" Mr. Wickham spoke softly, his eyes darting about at the growing ring of onlookers.

Elizabeth would not let him get away with confining this confrontation to the people who were close. Wanting the whole room to hear, she mustered a loud voice. "I saw the attack. Surely, my sister's grief would be reason enough not to grab her and kiss her, but not to let her go when she fought you and begged you to release her? That is not the behavior of a gentleman!"

This was met with startled gasps.

"You accuse me, but it is your sister who should decide if my attentions were welcome. You are exaggerating what happened. I let her go when she requested it."

As they'd anticipated, he didn't deny something had happened. Mr. Darcy had assured them Mr. Wickham liked to keep his lies close to the truth, to make them more believable. Mr. Darcy truly must know Mr. Wickham as well as Elizabeth had assured Jane.

"That's not what I saw," Elizabeth said.

Out of the corner of her eye, she saw her aunt step away. She could only assume the signal to collect Jane had been given.

"Why did you see anything? I was escorting Miss Bennet on a walk, the two of us. If you'll recall, I asked you to come along." Mr. Wickham leaned toward her. "What made you follow us? Jealousy?"

"Mistrust." Elizabeth had trouble keeping smugness from her voice. Mr. Wickham was behaving just as Darcy had anticipated. She hadn't appreciated until now what a fine observer of character Mr. Darcy was, or quite how clever. "I knew you were a liar, reason enough to mistrust you."

Elizabeth's aunt stepped back into the room. She hadn't been gone long enough to have found Jane, who didn't seem to be with her. Elizabeth hoped her aunt hadn't misunderstood her role.

"You knew I was a liar? When have I ever lied?" Mr. Wickham did a commendable job of sounding offended.

"The second time we ever spoke," Elizabeth said. She worked to keep her attention on the argument, not on her aunt. If Jane was going to be late, she needed to draw out the conversation as long as she could. "You told me you would never tell of your grievance against Mr. Darcy, yet you did."

"He told me that too," an officer in the crowd called out.

"I changed my mind." Mr. Wickham shrugged, looking unimpressed. "I made no promises."

"You changed your mind about the living left to you as well, didn't you? You asked for and received three thousand pounds to give it up," she countered. Where was Jane? Jane had said she would be there, and no matter how upset she was, she would keep her word. "You lied about a good and honorable man so people would feel sorry for you and so you could exact revenge on Mr. Darcy for not giving you both the living and the money."

"That didn't happen. Did Darcy tell you that?" Mr. Wickham's voice showed strain now and his eyes looked a bit wild.

"He did, and he offered confirmation from Colonel Fitzwilliam, who was with him," Elizabeth said. They had worked upon her wording, making it misleading but not a lie. It amused Elizabeth to fight Mr. Wickham on his own terms, in the realm of near truth.

"Darcy probably told that to Colonel Fitzwilliam some time ago to explain why the living went elsewhere. Fitzwilliam wouldn't doubt Darcy's word."

"And why wouldn't he? Because Mr. Darcy has never lied to him?" Elizabeth asked sweetly. "Did you ever lie to Colonel Fitzwilliam?"

"Of course not."

"You never told him Mr. Darcy was the one who threw stones at the parson's horse, not you?"

Mr. Wickham's eyes went wide. "That…that doesn't signify. I must have been only five or six then."

"Were you? Five or six?" Elizabeth knew he was lying about his age. Mr. Darcy had stated Mr. Wickham was eleven at the time. Mr. Darcy was sure Mr. Wickham would remember the incident, as he'd been caught and punished, which was unusual.

Mr. Wickham eyed her through narrowed lids. His lips pulled up in a smile. He looked around at the watching crowd. "I've always been attracted to Miss Bennet."

She wasn't surprised Mr. Wickham had abandoned refuting her accusations about his childhood. He couldn't know which lies she would counter, being unsure what details she possessed. He'd raised his voice when he spoke of Jane, obviously deciding to include the entire room in their conversation now, though everyone was already listening. All other talk had long since stilled.

"So you say," Elizabeth countered, wondering when Jane would appear and if Mr. Darcy and Mr. Bingley could hear Mr. Wickham from where they waited.

"Anyone who's seen her can understand why," Mr. Wickham continued in his stage voice.

There were some nods among the audience.

"She was so taken with Bingley, I knew I didn't have a chance. When I was alone with her, or so I thought, I was overcome. I wanted to care for her. She is so beautiful and sweet. A gentler soul has never walked this earth."

"Which is why you thought you could force me to marry you by saying you'd compromised me?" Jane said as she entered the room, drawing every eye. "You swine! How could you attempt to take such advantage of me, and in my grief? Elizabeth didn't tell me about you because she thought you deserved a chance to improve, but I think you may be beyond reformation."

Elizabeth hadn't thought any such thing, but she didn't mind Jane's improvisation. Trust her sister to want to make her seem good, even in the midst of a scene. She would set Jane straight later by admitting Mr. Wickham's nature had slipped her mind in the wake of their family's death.

"I think I need more of an explanation from you, Wickham," Colonel Forster said, his face grim.

"These girls are clearly deranged from the tragic deaths of their family." Mr. Wickham shook his head, affecting a pitying expression. "They are exaggerating a minor incident into an attack. I kissed a pretty girl. I asked her to marry me. What is the harm?"

There were some murmurs of agreement. Elizabeth fought not to scowl at those issuing them. What harm indeed!

"And what of maligning Mr. Darcy and lying?" Forster looked unsure, glancing from Elizabeth back to Mr. Wickham.

"Lies and delusions," Mr. Wickham declared in a strident voice.

"No, they are not," said Mr. Darcy.

He strode forward, his head clearly visible above the crowd, and Elizabeth had to admit he cut a striking figure. Mr. Wickham whipped around toward the sound of his voice. As the crowd parted for Mr. Darcy and Mr. Bingley, Mr. Wickham's face turned red.

"Mr. Wickham's acceptance of the three thousand pounds was done in the presence of two witnesses, both of whom also signed the same document he signed, giving up the living," Mr. Darcy said. He came to a halt before Mr. Wickham, Mr. Bingley at his side.

"Who are these witnesses? People you paid?" Mr. Wickham sneered, but he backed away from Mr. Darcy, running a shaking had through his hair.

"My attorney and Reverend Barnes, as you well know," Mr. Darcy countered. "I do pay my attorney, but Reverend Barnes happened to be visiting. Anyone who doubts can write them. That will make it three people and a signature against one."

A low buzzing filled the room as people whispered their opinions. Elizabeth couldn't make out any individual voices, but she was sure the room was on their side now.

"Wickham, I am waiting for an explanation," Colonel Forster said, his tone hard.

Mr. Wickham looked at him, opening his mouth and closing it again, no words uttered.

"Mr. Wickham, if you apologize to Miss Bennet and admit you lied about her, I will not sue you for slander," Mr. Darcy said. "If word reaches me you ever malign any young lady, I will sue you. I may not be able to collect anything, because I believe your debts outweigh your assets, but if you ever come into money, I will see my debt is collected, even if it costs me more to collect it than it is worth. If you don't ever come into money, something tells me you don't want to garner the attentions of the court."

Mr. Wickham took another step back. He turned wide eyes on Jane. "Miss Bennet, I was wrong. I apologize."

"You lied," Mr. Bingley said through gritted teeth, echoing Elizabeth's thoughts.

"I lied." Mr. Wickham cast a fearful look at his colonel.

"And now there is the issue of your debts in Meryton," Elizabeth's Uncle Phillips said. "I believe the tally is easily more than the minimum to send you to debtors' prison. I would be happy to buy your debts and start the process."

Mr. Wickham bolted.

Chapter Six

After giving Elizabeth and Miss Bennet a few days to collect themselves, Darcy and Bingley called at the Phillips to see how they were handling the aftermath of the scene at Lucas Lodge. They both looked well enough and both had ready smiles, though those were still shadowed by sorrow. Darcy liked to think Elizabeth's greeting for him was warmer than the one she offered Bingley. There could be no doubt the ones exchanged by Bingley and Miss Bennet were as enthusiastic as the subdued nature of recent events allowed.

"I should like to take a walk," Miss Bennet said once greetings were exchanged.

Darcy saw the startled look Elizabeth gave her sister. He was surprised as well. He would have thought Miss Bennet not kindly disposed toward walks for a time.

"Are you certain?" Elizabeth asked.

"I am. I should like to walk the same path as I took with Mr. Wickham."

Now even Bingley looked surprised.

"It truly is a beautiful place to walk," Miss Bennet said. "He wasn't lying about Lydia loving it there, for she'd told me the same thing. That's why I agreed to go with him." She gave Darcy a sad smile. "As you said, he fills his lies with truth to make them believable."

Darcy nodded. "He does."

"I should like to have good memories to replace the bad ones, so I won't fear walking in one of Lydia's favorite places," Miss Bennet said.

Elizabeth scrutinized her sister for a moment before nodding. "Then that is what we shall do."

Elizabeth and Miss Bennet retrieved their bonnets and the four of them set out. Miss Bennet, walking beside Bingley, seemed inclined to hurry. Darcy lengthened his stride. He was a bit startled to feel Elizabeth's hand touch his arm. He looked down to find her smiling up at him.

"It's too fine a day for such a quick pace," she murmured.

Darcy raised his eyebrows but slowed. What Elizabeth said made complete sense. It was a fine day, and he had no need to chaperone Bingley, nor to be chaperoned while with Elizabeth. In fact, as they left town, he realized this was the first time he'd been alone with her in far too long.

"Miss Elizabeth," he said, proffering his arm. "The road is less even here."

"Thank you," she said, availing herself of his support.

Her hand on his coat sleeve brought her noticeably nearer. She smelled faintly of rose petals and the promise of spring. As they walked, her skirts brushed his leg. He wanted to stop and face her so he could read her eyes. He longed to ask her if her opinion of him had altered in any encouraging way. He wondered if she'd noticed how he'd reformed himself.

"I'm glad you and Mr. Bingley found your way through the kitchen to approach from the other direction so Mr. Wickham couldn't see you until it was too late," Elizabeth said. "I never thought of you as someone who would be willing to go through a kitchen."

He affected an easy shrug, surprised her thoughts were so parallel to his own. "I am not above kitchens. Your uncle was magnificent."

"He was. I've underrated him." She glanced up at him.

"I have as well." He'd also underrated Mr. Phillips on his handling of his wife. She responded to his patience by being a better person than her deceased sister ever was.

"Thank you for all of your help. I think Jane will recover from what happened without too much difficulty."

"I believe Bingley would like to help in that recovery."

"And you will permit it?"

"I will support it."

Her eyes dropped, but he could see her smile. She gently steered him from the road and up an unused looking path. Though it wasn't strictly proper, he didn't protest. He wondered if it was the same one Wickham had taken and they would find Bingley and Miss Bennet ahead. He rather hoped not.

"Allow me to apologize to you for misjudging your family," he said.

"Then allow me to admit you did not completely misjudge them. Did you know my aunt sent a servant to summon Jane? It was a servant she knew well and knew would complete the task, but it was her one role to play, and an important one, yet she didn't see to it herself."

"I did not know, but I had wondered why she was in the room when we arrived."

"She didn't want to miss the spectacle. She's a gossip." Elizabeth sighed.

"I will admit I may not have thought much of your aunt in the past, but she played her part well. Sending the servant was almost cunning. It would have looked odd to Wickham if he'd noticed her departure."

Elizabeth laughed. "You found the good in someone in a manner worthy of Jane, Mr. Darcy."

"I shall take that as high praise."

She cast him an amused look, but it disappeared as she turned her eyes back to the path they walked. Though she engaged in light laughter and gentle smiles, Darcy could still feel the sorrow enshrouding her. He wished their relationship was of a closer nature, so he could offer her the comfort of his arms to ward off some small portion of her grief, or speak in low tones of his parents' deaths, sharing the small amount of wisdom he possessed on such matters.

"Mr. Darcy, I never apologized for misjudging you so completely and for the harshness of our final exchange in Kent."

That sounded like progress for his cause. Perhaps they were closer to him offering comfort than he'd dared hope. "Your statement yesterday is apology enough."

"My statement?"

"That I am a good and honorable man."

A blush touched her cheeks. "You are those things, as you well know. You do not need my confirmation of it."

He stopped walking. Elizabeth turned, her eyes questioning. He caught her hand in his as it slid from his arm. They were quite alone now. He couldn't hear any sounds of humanity, not even Bingley and Miss Bennet. There was only the sound of a light breeze and the trill of birds.

"Forgive me for saying as much, but you are wrong," he said. "I do need your confirmation of it. Yours more than anyone's."

Elizabeth looked up at him through luminous eyes. He reached for her other hand. She didn't protest, further raising his hopes.

"It is really too soon to say anything, I know," he said. "Yet I cannot pass this moment by. You were magnificent in your handling of Wickham, and before a room filled with people no less. Everything I have seen of you since returning to Hertfordshire only stands to confirm I was as right to propose to you as I was wrong in how I went about it. I was also egregiously wrong in my expectations as to your answer. My feelings…well, my feelings have changed." He took in the hurt surprise in her expression and hurried on, realizing he was once again making a poor showing. "That is, I love you just as much, or more, but I admire you so much more. Please don't be upset about the impropriety of proposing so soon after your family's deaths. I can wait a long time for an answer."

She stared at him. Tears shimmered in her eyes. His heart stopped mid-beat. He'd frightened her when he said his feelings had changed. He hadn't meant to, but maybe her sorrow had clarified to her that she wanted his love, or maybe his blundering words had driven her further away. He almost dreaded learning which, for fear of the latter.

"You don't need to wait," she finally said. A smile curved her lips. "I was a fool to believe Mr. Wickham, but I would be a greater fool by far if I let you get away."

Darcy pulled her to him, their lips meeting. Throwing propriety to the wind, he reveled in her kisses, not caring that anyone might come up the path. He'd waited too long to hold her to stop now. He wanted desperately to kiss away her sorrow.

"Ahem."

Darcy recognized the voice as Bingley's. Reluctantly, he set Elizabeth away from him, but took one of her hands in his. "Bingley," he said, affecting a cool tone. From the corner of his eye, he could see the redness sufficing Elizabeth's face, but he could also glimpse her smile.

"Darcy," Bingley said, looking amused.

Darcy noticed Bingley was holding Miss Bennet's hand. She, too, was blushing. Taking in her slightly disheveled appearance, he didn't think her coloring was entirely due to stumbling upon him kissing her sister. It appeared Miss Bennet had created some of the pleasant memories she'd sought. "Time to return to town?" Darcy suggested.

"I imagine so," Bingley said.

"Yes," Elizabeth said. "I think we'd best. I believe Uncle Phillips has a busy evening ahead of him. We wouldn't want to add to that by worrying him with tardiness."

Pleased he now had a lifetime to ensure Elizabeth's happiness, Darcy settled her hand on his arm and led the way back to Meryton.

Epilogue

Mr. Phillips sat down at his desk to write Mr. Gardiner.

My Dear Brother Edward,
Do not be alarmed at receiving another letter from me. I have no tragedy to report, unless you consider it a tragedy Jane and Elizabeth won't be with you in London this coming winter. Jane is engaged to Mr. Bingley. You've heard about him and I'm sure you will approve of him when you meet him. Elizabeth surprised all of us by accepting a proposal from Mr. Darcy.

Mr. Phillips put down his pen. He wasn't certain how much Mr. Gardiner knew about Darcy and needed to think on how to describe him favorably but not fawningly. He picked up his glass of port and took a sip, reflecting on the past few days.

Yes, Elizabeth had surprised them all. If he was possessed of any level of perception, and his wife was to be believed, Elizabeth hadn't cared for Mr. Darcy when he'd first been in Hertfordshire. Now she'd enthusiastically agreed to a proposal from him, and Darcy was talking about inviting him and his wife to Pemberley. It amused Mr. Phillips to think of how his wife would behave in Darcy's grand home, but he would visit them because he would miss Elizabeth. Fortunately, he would be able to see Jane often.

Mr. Phillips was pleased he knew his niece well enough to see her affection for Darcy was genuine. Although he could see the glowing happiness of both his nieces oftentimes disappeared when they remembered their families, he hoped time and love would help heal their grief. He smiled, knowing both his nieces were wedding good men.

Good men, but ones not overly familiar with the law. Mr. Phillips was moderately sure Mr. Darcy had no notion of how short the statute of limitations was for slander. With any luck, Mr. Wickham's education was similarly lacking. He wondered if he should advise Mr. Bingley to buy up Wickham's debts, in case he ever needed insurance against Wickham slandering Jane's name.

Perhaps it would be unnecessary, since reports had it Mr. Wickham had left Lucas Lodge to go immediately to his quarters and gather his possessions. There was even a rumor that another officer had a small stash of money that had disappeared. Wickham had also disappeared, and Mr. Phillips doubted they would hear from him again. He was probably trying to get used to another name, even though the theft could likely never be proven. The debts could be, and that was enough.

Mr. Phillips took another sip of port, his attention wandering over the papers arranged on his desk. Aside from the letter, he had another task to attend to: drawing up a new will. There was less money than before. The five thousand pounds he'd added to Mr. Bennet's meager savings had decreased his worth.

Not by much, however. In spite of them finding wealthy husbands, he was still pleased with the deception he'd practiced in increasing Jane's and Elizabeth's funds. He hadn't wanted his nieces to go through life feeling bitter toward their father. Let them believe he'd provided for them. No one ever need learn he hadn't.

Not even Mrs. Phillips. She'd found one of his secret bank accounts, but the other two remained hidden. He recalled Mr. Bingley's sister boasting about her dowry. Her superciliousness had momentarily tempted him to allow rumor of his wealth to surface, but he'd quelled the desire. It was a pity he would never find out the reaction when his will was read, and his worth discovered.

In spite of their obvious lack of need, he was still going to will his money to his nieces. Though, he should leave something to the Gardiner children as well. Making it per stirpes, not per capita, would mean his two favorite nieces would share half of what was left.

He would put the money in trust and allow Mrs. Phillips to live off the interest but give her no way to touch the principal, since he didn't trust his wife with money. Years ago, when Mr. Phillips had taken over the law firm from old Mr. Gardiner, he'd promised he would take care of the man's daughter, and he did. It saddened Mr. Phillips they didn't have any children, but fate had compensated his pain at that loss by giving him Jane and Elizabeth. He was glad he was able to help them.

Setting his port aside, Mr. Phillips returned to writing his letter, a much happier one than the last, smiling all the while.

~ The End ~

Miss Bingley's Christmas

A Christmas Tale

Part One: Christmas Eve

It wasn't freezing, which was good, because Miss Bingley didn't want the flowers she'd purchased to freeze, but it was quite cold. She and her sister, Louisa Hurst, were on their way back from a new flower market. It wasn't in the best of neighborhoods, but it had lived up to the rumor of splendid blooms. Normally, Miss Bingley wouldn't set foot in the part of town they were in, but tomorrow wasn't a normal day. It was Christmas. More importantly, Mr. Darcy and his sister were joining the Hursts and Miss Bingley for Christmas dinner.

Miss Bingley leaned forward, peeking past the heavy curtains draping the coach windows. The thick fabric provided privacy and blocked out some of the chill, but left it rather dark within. Not that the world without offered much to brighten things, for the day was overcast. She sighed, letting the drapes fall back into place. She'd been doing everything imaginable to make sure dinner tomorrow would be flawless.

It couldn't be, though, for it wasn't at Pemberley. Miss Bingley had long since realized nothing could be perfect if it didn't involve Mr. Darcy's marvelous estate, and his formidable fortune. That included her future. Christmas at Pemberley, as they'd originally planned, would have brought that future much nearer, she was sure of it. Were she in his home at so celebrated a time of year, behaving with perfection, he would have seen how right it was to have her there.

Sadly, Christmas at Pemberley was not slated for that year, in spite of plans and hopes. Miss Darcy had been ill for several weeks. She was now on the mend, but Mr. Darcy had proclaimed it impossible to remove her from London for the time being. He did not feel a journey would improve her, and he wished to keep her near the best doctors England had to offer. Miss Bingley supposed she should be grateful Miss Darcy was as recovered as he reported, or Mr. Darcy might have kept her sequestered and remained by her side.

"Caroline, do stop twisting your mouth into that horrendous expression," Louisa said, eyeing her from the opposite seat. "What if someone should see you?"

Miss Bingley resisted the urge to show her older sister an even less pleasant expression, smoothing her features instead. "No one can see us inside the coach with the curtains drawn."

"But you may forget you've permitted the expression, or form a habit of it."

Reminding herself that Louisa was under a greater strain than usual, suspecting she was finally with child, Miss Bingley forwent replying.

"At least the flowers lived up to expectation," Louisa said after a time, folding her hands in her lap. "Although we were forced to enter such a wretched part of town, I'm not certain it was worth the journey."

"I am," Miss Bingley said. "Everything must be just so, tomorrow. It's Christmas, after all, and--"

A terrible crashing sound ricocheted down the street. It seemed to come from somewhere ahead of them. Before Miss Bingley could pull back the curtain to look, their carriage came to an abrupt halt, tossing her toward Louisa.

Miss Bingley flung out her arms, bracing them on either side of her sister so they wouldn't collide. Her face quite near Louisa's, it was easy to see how pale she was. Miss Bingley pushed herself back into her seat just as another crash sounded somewhere behind them. Reflexively, she looked over her shoulder, though they were enclosed in the carriage.

"Are you injured?" she asked, turning back to Louisa. Her sister was testing the back of her head with one hand, her free arm wrapped protectively about her middle.

Louisa shook her head, but her lips were a thin line and her color was poor.

A knock sounded and the carriage door was thrown open, letting in the dusky afternoon light. Miss Bingley pulled back, but the silhouette in the doorway quickly resolved itself into one of Mr. Hurst's footmen. Miss Bingley forced herself to draw a calming breath. It wouldn't do to appear ruffled before a servant.

"Are you harmed, missus, miss?" the man asked, cold air sweeping in around him.

Resisting the urge to shiver, she glanced at Louisa, but her sister's lips were pressed closed. "We're well," Miss Bingley offered, hoping it was true. "Is there a difficulty?"

"Two carts have run afoul of one another, miss, right in front of the carriage. They look right tangled, too. I'm on my way to see if we can back up." He pointed behind them.

"Carry on, then," Miss Bingley said. "Report what you find."

"Yes, miss." Closing the door, the footman disappeared.

Silence descended on the interior of the carriage. Louisa stopped rubbing her head, but her color didn't improve. Miss Bingley worked not to bite her lower lip, worried for her sister's delicate condition. Perhaps the perfect flowers to decorate for Mr. Darcy weren't worth it after all. From somewhere ahead of them, she could hear equine cries of distress and men shouting. A similar raucous was discernable behind. Always proper, Miss Bingley did not go to the window to gawk, waiting patiently instead.

After what seemed like half an age, the door opened to reveal Mr. Hurst's footman. "It isn't pretty out here, missus, miss," he said. "The street in front is blocked off. Them two carts were going faster than they ought, and hit on a slick patch. There's a broken axel as sure as I know my own name, and one of the horses is down."

Miss Bingley nodded, wishing he would speak more quickly. All warmth was leaving the inside of the carriage with the door open. Across from her, Louisa shivered. "And behind?"

"A wagon overturned, miss, and a good thing, too." He bobbing his head along with his words. "It's blocking the way back, but it tipped itself avoiding us when we stopped so quick like, so I can't complain. Spewed cargo all over the street, though. It'll be a time getting it all sorted."

"Thank you for the report," Miss Bingley said.

"No trouble, miss. I'll go see if I can help clear the way."

They waited, the silence inside the carriage punctuated by the yelling and arguing of masculine voices without. Though it was obvious she was trying to suppress it, Louisa continued to shiver. Miss Bingley bit her lower lip. There was no denying it was getting colder.

There was a knock and the door opened again, revealing the footman. "Missus, miss," he said. "We're having a bit of trouble out here. If it's not too forward of me, miss, I know them flowers you purchased are important. I'm conversant with the way back and can have them there in half an hour, if I step smart. You've the coachman to see you home, once the way is clear. Shall I take the blooms before the cold ruins them?"

Miss Bingley looked to Louisa, who shrugged. She turned back to the footman. "Yes, if you please. I shall mention your dedication to Mr. Hurst."

"Thank you, miss," he said.

It was only after the footman left that Miss Bingley realized he would soon be sitting by a warm fire while they remained in the cold carriage. What other choice was there, though? She didn't wish to make her way that far through the streets, and she couldn't ask Louisa to, not in her condition.

The male arguing continued, and the temperature inside the carriage inched lower. They'd left with warm bricks, but those had long since cooled. Miss Bingley knocked on the roof, to get the driver's attention, but no one came. Finally, forgoing her dignity, she pulled open the curtain and stuck her head out the window.

Though she didn't know what the street before and behind had looked like at the moment of the accidents, it was obvious they weren't near to being cleared. She spotted Mr. Hurst's driver on the street behind, arguing with a stout, shabbily clad man. With a shudder, she pulled her head in and the curtains closed.

"We should be able to make it ourselves," Miss Bingley said, coming to a decision. "They don't appear to be progressing with freeing our carriage and it's only getting colder, and nearer dark. We can't stay here." It would be a bit of a walk for Louisa, but moving would warm her. It was obvious from her sister's tremors that sitting in the cold carriage wasn't doing her any good.

"Mr. Hurst's carriage, we can't leave it."

"The coachman will stay." After all, he was the one who'd manage to put them in such dreadful conditions, by choosing that street. If someone must stay, he should.

"Do you know the way?" Louisa asked, twin lines of worry marring her brow.

"Not entirely, but I can ask." She knew the location of the part of town they were in, mostly in an effort to avoid it. It should be simple enough to return to nearby areas she was familiar with.

They climbed out, the cold wind giving Miss Bingley momentary pause. Though overcast, it appeared later even than she'd expected, but that spurred her on. She and Louisa were not spending all evening in a freezing carriage in a less than savory part of town. Not when a mere thirty minute walk would alleviate the circumstance.

Leaving Louisa by the carriage, Miss Bingley approached the driver and acquired directions, reminding him it was his duty to see the carriage home. Mr. Hurst's driver was properly deferential, but the man he'd been arguing with had an unsavory face. Miss Bingley hurried back to her sister and took her arm, leading her away.

She thought she'd memorized the directions, but soon realized she was completely lost. She didn't admit as much to Louisa, not wanting to strain her spirits. Miss Bingley wasn't certain how far they'd walked, but she was sure they'd soon be someplace she recognized. Then she would guide Louisa home.

A carriage sped by, spewing them with the dirty slush from the road and eliciting a small cry of anguish from Louisa. Before long, Miss Bingley's fingers and toes were numb. Her hem was heavy with water and her shoes squished with each step. To make matters worse, it started snowing. The snow melted on her head and shoulders, dampening her hat, hair and dress and making her shiver. She drew her sister nearer, trying to provide any small amount of warmth and shelter she could. Louisa was white and trembling.

"Miss Bingley? Is that you?"

The voice came from somewhere behind them. Miss Bingley stopped walking, blinking lashes heavy with melted snowflakes. Had she imagined the call? The voice was familiar, but whose?

"Miss Bingley, do you require assistance?"

Turning Louisa with her, Miss Bingley spun to see a modish carriage stopped on the opposite side of the street. The curtain was pulled back. Miss Jane Bennet's angelic face peeked out.

"Miss Bennet," Miss Bingley cried, relief flooding her. Here, at least, was a face she knew, and a kind one at that. "Thank goodness. We're lost. Perhaps you can take us home."

She set out across the street, steadying Louisa as she stumbled in the middle of the roadway. A footman jumped down from the back of the carriage, running to her sister's side. It was a testament to how unwell Louisa was that she didn't protest the man taking her other arm.

Miss Bennet threw the door open, jumping out. "Are you well, Mrs. Hurst?"

"Yes, thank you," Louisa stammered, her lips blue-tinged. "Simply cold."

"We must get you both somewhere warm immediately," Miss Bennet said, taking the footman's place at Louisa's side. "Thank you, Gregory," she added, giving the servant a smile as she guided Louisa to the carriage door.

Miss Bingley suppressed a grimace at Miss Bennet's crass behavior; noticing a servant and addressing him by name. It wouldn't do to pull faces at their savior. "A lift would be much appreciated. We live on Grosvenor Street."

"That isn't very close," a voice inside the carriage said as Miss Bennet helped Louisa inside. "We're less than five minutes from where we're staying. We should take you there and get you warm and dry. Then we can see about getting you home."

Miss Bingley winced. She knew that voice. Elizabeth Bennet. Were Louisa not already inside the carriage and not so terribly pale, Miss Bingley would insist they keep walking. Miss Jane Bennet was pretty, sweet and tolerable. Her only flaw was that it had taken Miss Bingley considerable effort to wrench her brother back from pursing a disastrous union between them. Elizabeth Bennet was by far worse. She was distressingly strong willed, oddly alluring to men in general and, most horribly, to Mr. Darcy in particular. Miss Bingley couldn't think of anyone worse to meet in London.

Miss Bennet stepped up into the carriage, leaving Miss Bingley standing in the doorway. As her eyes adjusted to the dimness of the interior, she realized there was an unfamiliar occupant. Miss Bennet quickly introduced Miss Bingley and her sister to Mrs. Gardiner. Miss Bingley instantly recalled the Bennet sisters had an aunt from London whose husband was in trade. Judging from the smartness of their conveyance, they were successful in whatever business they were in. While people in trade were vulgar by nature, they could often afford fine things. Miss Bingley should know. Her father had been in trade.

The Bennet sisters had Louisa between them, appearing quite solicitous of her pallor and shivering. Miss Bingley knew there was nothing for it but to climb in and seat herself beside Mrs. Gardiner. At least she would be out of the wind and snow, no longer walking about the streets.

As soon as she was settled, Mrs. Gardiner tapped on the roof and they set out. Miss Bingley started to arrange her skirt, but stopped when she realized it was pointless. Her numb fingers were doing a poor job of it, and her sodden hem was unresponsive. Folding her hands in her lap, she turned to Mrs. Gardiner, realizing she hadn't yet dispensed with the appropriate courtesy. "Thank you for taking us up in your carriage, Mrs. Gardiner."

"It is no trouble, Miss Bingley. It's a pleasure to meet you."

Miss Bingley suppressed a wince. The conventional pleasantry seemed somehow undeserved after how she'd helped persuade her and Louisa's brother, Charles, not to marry Miss Bennet, but treating it as anything more than a normal polite remark would be tantamount to admitting guilt. She didn't feel guilty. She'd done what she must to protect Charles and secure both of their futures, for what sort of match could she hope for if her brother married so far beneath them?

"Whatever were you doing out walking?" Miss Bennet asked before Miss Bingley could recover enough to turn the subject to taking them home.

"We were at the flower market," Louisa said, her teeth chattering as she spoke. Miss Bingley prayed she wouldn't mention why. "Our carriage was boxed in by accidents on the street. We thought we must walk or freeze."

"How awful," Miss Bennet said, looking sincerely disturbed on their behalf.

"Surely you didn't set out without knowing the way?" Miss Elizabeth asked, frowning.

"I asked directions of our coachman. They were obviously incorrect," Miss Bingley said, sitting up as straight as she could with her damp dress weighing her down. She wouldn't admit fault in front of Miss Elizabeth, who was always seeking it in her.

Miss Elizabeth raised her eyebrows, but didn't open her mouth.

"We walked for ages, and then someone drove by and drenched us with water from the street," Louisa lamented.

"People can be terribly supercilious," Miss Elizabeth murmured.

"Yes, well, about taking us home, I really think Louisa should be gotten into a warm house and dry clothing immediately," Miss Bingley said.

"And so she shall be," Mrs. Gardiner said. "We're only a turn away from my home. You're both welcome there."

"Thank you," Louisa said with such relief that Miss Bingley clamped her mouth closed over her protest.

She leaned back, assessing her shivering sister once more. Louisa was uncertain, but she'd confided several days ago that she was likely with child. It would be her and Mr. Hurst's first. An unfamiliar feeling of responsibility assailed Miss Bingley. She couldn't force her sister to remain cold, wet and shaking for any longer than necessary. She would have to concede to entering the home of a couple who not only were in trade, but were relatives of Miss Elizabeth.

"We've arrived," Mrs. Gardiner said, smiling, as the carriage slowed.

Miss Bennet disembarked first, turning back to help Louisa, though the footman was in attendance. Miss Bingley had to admit, at least to herself, that it was touching how solicitous Miss Bennet was. They hadn't treated Miss Bennet as amiably as they could have, yet she seemed honestly worried for Louisa and desirous of helping her.

Miss Bingley got out next, followed by Mrs. Gardiner and Miss Elizabeth. Raising her gaze to the building Miss Bennet was leading her sister into, Miss Bingley conceded it was a respectable enough looking home. Following them inside, she soon saw the interior was at least bearable. Being honest with herself, she could grant it was considerably more spacious than the Hursts' home on Grosvenor Street. Of course, the Hursts lived in a much more fashionable neighborhood, and one had to pay in coin or space, whichever one could afford.

Mrs. Gardiner took charge in a competent manner, calling for baths to be drawn and tea served, and arranging for word of their trials to be sent to Mr. Hurst. Soon, they were all seated in a cozy parlor, warm tea in hand. Louisa seemed somewhat revived, but still shivered. Worried for her, Miss Bingley insisted her sister bathe first. Miss Bingley's shivering had stopped almost immediately upon entering the warm home, and it wasn't as much a chore as she'd imagined it would be to talk pleasantly with Mrs. Gardiner and the Bennet sisters.

Eventually, Miss Bingley had her turn at a bath and finally felt truly warm. After, she descended to the drawing room, wearing a dress she recognized as belonging to Miss Elizabeth. It was a bit too short for her, but not indecently so. What bothered her most was that it was totally unfashionable. No, that wasn't true. What bothered her most was she was now beholden to Elizabeth Bennet. Louisa was wearing a dress Miss Bingley had seen on Miss Bennet on multiple occasions. It was equally unfashionable. Somehow, it looked nicer on Miss Bennet than on Louisa.

Settling into the drawing room with the others, Miss Bingley soon found she and Louisa were not being accorded the respect they were due. Mrs. Gardiner should be honored to have them as company, but she didn't act honored. She acted hospitable. Miss Bingley and Louisa moved in the highest society. Mrs. Gardiner ought to make an effort to express how elevating it was to be in their company. Oh, Mrs. Gardiner listened politely when Louisa mentioned some of the people she knew, but only asked enough questions for minimal politeness. She wasn't truly interested.

They were interrupted by a manservant whose face was red from cold and who hadn't shed his snow-covered cape. He handed Mrs. Gardiner a letter. "Mr. Hurst sent this back with me, missus," he said, before backing from the room.

"Thank you, Daniel," Mrs. Gardiner murmured. She handed the letter to Louisa. "It's addressed to you, Mrs. Hurst."

"Thank you." Louisa took the letter, opening it to scan the words. She glanced at Miss Bingley, then dropped her gaze back to the page. "It says, we were very worried when the carriage came back without you and your sister. The weather is foul. Mrs. Gardiner wrote that both of you can spend the night there and Bingley and I are welcome to come to dinner tomorrow, and may invite the Darcys. I don't want to subject you or your sister to more of this terrible weather. We will see you tomorrow." Louisa folded the note, turning to Mrs. Gardiner. "Inviting Mr. Hurst, Charles and the Darcys was very kind of you. If you had asked, I would have told you it was unnecessary."

"Think nothing of it," Mrs. Gardiner said. "It's our pleasure to have you all for Christmas dinner, and to have you both with us this evening."

"Thank you," Louisa repeated. She shivered. "I was not looking forward to braving the weather."

Miss Bingley drew in a deep breath. Did she imagine the smugness in Mrs. Gardiner's tone, or the happy way she glanced at Miss Bennet? There was no missing Miss Bennet's blush, though she had her face downturned.

Miss Bingley couldn't believe she would be forced to spend the night there, and without her own things. She would be forced to wear this dress all evening and tomorrow, at least until Mr. Hurst arrived. Would he think to bring anything for them? He was notoriously inept when it came to his wife. Should she try to get a letter to him? Better, she could insist a carriage be called to take them home.

Miss Bingley glanced at the window, but the curtains were drawn. The letter-bearing servant had been quite covered in snow. Mr. Hurst must realize how wretched it was to make them remain at the Gardiners. He wouldn't advise it were it not necessary. Miss Bingley might go, but she couldn't ask Louisa to in her condition, and wouldn't abandon her there.

Maybe she would be able to make the whole incident into an amusing story, to regale her peers with. Miss Bigley suppressed a sigh. It didn't seem funny now. Could it be in retrospect? No. She wouldn't tell anyone about where she was spending Christmas Eve.

Not simply Christmas Eve but, from Mr. Hurst's letter, Christmas day. Worse, Mrs. Gardiner had invited the Darcys. Miss Bingley could only hope Mr. Darcy would decline. He couldn't want to spend Christmas in a house owned by people in trade. He must realize from the address that the place was far too low for him and Miss Darcy.

Miss Bingley looked about the well-appointed room, cheerfully festooned with pine boughs and ribbon. It didn't look like a low place. Did she not know it to be, she wouldn't suspect.

There was a commotion in the hall and the room was suddenly flooded with children. Miss Bingley steeled herself, going through the proper introductions. She didn't dislike children, of course, hoping to have some of her own eventually. She was sure the children of people in trade would be horribly vulgar, though, and didn't want to encourage them to remain to shock her and Louisa with their lack of manners.

It turned out she needn't have worried. The Gardiner children were quite civilized. Furthermore, they seemed to prefer interacting with their aunts to addressing Miss Bingley or Louisa. Like their mother, they didn't seem to understand the good that could come of connecting with people of quality. Miss Bingley supposed it was part of the reason people remained in such low states. They didn't have a proper enough understanding of the world to take advantage of such opportunities.

When Mr. Gardiner came home, he too was covered in snow, a fact he rectified after introductions. When he reappeared, looking nearly fashionable, he took a seat beside his wife. She smiled at him with a warmth Miss Bingley deemed not entirely appropriate. People in her circle would never be so vulgar as to show it if they cared for their spouse.

"You're later than usual," Mrs. Gardiner said, but there was no reproach in her tone.

"I let everyone go home early, it being Christmas Eve," Mr. Gardiner said. "I stayed to wrap up any little things left undone." He cast a glance toward the curtained windows. "I was the best choice, as I was so near home. Still, the walk took me three times what it normally would. It's beastly out there. I saw several carriages stuck and wasn't passed by a single one actually managing to move. I hope all of the servants are in for the night?"

"They are, though I gathered Daniel had a time of getting back from the Hursts."

Shortly thereafter, the children retired and dinner was served. To Miss Bingley's relief, the meal was quite good. Seated between Mr. Gardiner and Miss Bennet, the conversation was tolerable. No, she had to admit, it was pleasant. Mr. Gardiner didn't bring his business to the meal, and was well-bred and well informed. After dinner, she had an enjoyable conversation with Mrs. Gardiner. She may not know the people Miss Bingley knew, but she was very up to date on fashion.

Part Two: Christmas Day

The next morning, Caroline woke up in a borrowed nightgown and a borrowed bed. She stretched, oddly relaxed. It was obvious the storm of the evening before had passed. In the gap where the curtains met, she could see a wall of snow piled up on the sill, but sunlight streamed through above. Turning her head in the other direction, Caroline found Louisa still asleep, curled on her side as she'd always slept when they were children.

It was strange to think of herself as Caroline, rather than Miss Bingley. Perhaps it was sharing the room with her sister and using first names. She stared up at the sun-touched ceiling, thinking about the day ahead. It occurred to her that, as she wasn't at the Hursts preparing for Christmas dinner, she had nothing to worry about. Until the gentlemen arrived, there wasn't even anyone to impress. The Gardiners were very pleasant, but their opinion of her didn't matter and she was unlikely to see them again after today.

Today. It was Christmas. Perhaps that was why she was so relaxed.

They attended an early morning service at a church which was a block away. Someone had shoveled the path the entire way, which made it bearable to walk there. She and Louisa had done each other's hair. Louisa wasn't as skilled at it as Caroline was, but she didn't mind the lopsided results. There was something pleasant about her older sister fussing over her hair, as Louisa used to when they were young. Their clothing had been washed but wasn't dry, so Caroline wore Miss Elizabeth's dress from the day before and a totally unfashionable cloak Mrs. Gardiner offered her. She was glad she was unlikely to know anyone in the small church, consoling herself that she was unlikely to be recognized.

When they returned, Miss Bennet and Miss Elizabeth said they would spend time with the children. They disappeared into the nursery, leaving Caroline and Louisa to entertain their host and hostess. Yet, Caroline found herself entertained. The Gardiners were even more pleasant, knowledgeable and intelligent than the day before. It took Caroline some time to realize the change wasn't in them, but in her.

She was happier without the Bennet sisters present. She was free of the jealousy she felt for Miss Elizabeth over Mr. Darcy. More than that, she was relieved of an emotion she hadn't until now realized she harbored in their presence, envy. Caroline was envious of Miss Bennet. Envious of her serene beauty and inner core of strength. Miss Bennet had none of the uncertainties that Caroline did. She felt no shame for her relatives in trade and could rejoice at being a gentleman's daughter.

"I should apprise you, Mr. Darcy sent word this morning that he and Miss Darcy will join Mr. Hurst and Mr. Bingley in dining with us today," Mrs. Gardiner said, breaking into Caroline's musings.

"That's pleasant news, isn't it Caroline?" Louisa said, giving her a conspiratorial look.

Caroline offered a smile, but she could have spared Louisa her hopes. With Miss Elizabeth around, Mr. Darcy wouldn't be awarding Caroline any attention. "Yes, pleasant indeed."

"We will also be joined by Mr. Taylor," Mr. Gardiner said.

"Mr. Taylor?" Louisa repeated and Caroline could hear the worry in her sister's tone, for the man couldn't possibly be suitable company.

"He married my younger sister, who died in childbirth nearly two years ago," Mrs. Gardiner said. Her tone was touched with sorrow, but she smiled at them. "I'm hoping he will take an interest in one of my nieces. He needs someone to take care of the children, both the baby and his older daughter. He would make either of my nieces a good husband."

"Yes, of course," Louisa said, sounding relieved.

Miss Elizabeth appeared in the doorway. "I'm afraid we've worn the children out," she said, her easy smile sparking new envy in Caroline. "They're being put down for their nap. Jane has gone to change for dinner, and I shall join her."

"Very well, dear," Mrs. Gardiner said.

Miss Elizabeth cast a pleasant look about the room and disappeared down the hall.

Louisa stood. "I'm sure my gown is dry by now. I shall go check. Coming, Caroline?"

"My dress is much heavier. I doubt it's ready, but should stay near the hearth a while longer. I'll join you shortly." Caroline didn't want to accompany her sister. She knew Louisa would take the opportunity to complain about the Gardiners, going over every detail of their conversation. For once, Caroline didn't feel like joining in, or even listening to her complaints.

Louisa blinked once, looking surprised, before nodding. "Until later, then," she said, leaving.

"I, too, must make myself respectable," Mr. Gardiner said, leaving Caroline and Mrs. Gardiner alone.

With a smile, Mrs. Gardiner turned to Caroline. "Miss Bingley, I imagine you've had the advantage of the best schools. May I ask, though it is still some ways in my elder daughter's future, where did you attend and what are your thoughts on the education you received there?"

Caroline had indeed received an excellent education and was more than happy to oblige Mrs. Gardiner's curiosity. When the Bennet sisters returned, they listened politely to her description of the lessons in music, drawing, literature, deportment and language. Caroline stopped midsentence when the door knocker was heard. Surely it was too early for Mr. Darcy and the others to arrive.

A tall, strikingly handsome man was shown into the parlor. He was impeccably dressed, though his casual stance and somewhat ruffled hair gave the impression his attire was the work of a caring valet and not of his own impetuous. Caroline stood along with the others, thinking that either of the Bennet sisters would be foolish to pass up the opportunity to promote themselves to the man, assuming this was Mr. Taylor come to call.

He bowed and Caroline belatedly noticed a small child stood beside him, holding his hand. She looked about four and bore some resemblance both to Mrs. Gardiner and to the Gardiner children. She wore a pretty dress and was properly beribboned for Christmas. Caroline couldn't help but smile at her. Greetings were exchanged all round, revealing that this was indeed Mrs. Gardiner's bother by marriage, Mr. Taylor.

"You're very welcome Joseph and Mary," Mr. Gardiner said. He held out his arms to the little girl. "Merry Christmas, my dear."

Mary started forward eagerly enough, but her eyes roamed over the assembled adults, most of whom Caroline assumed she did not know, and she stopped. She stood for a moment, her round little face overcome with uncertainty, then turned back to her father and clutched his leg. He picked her up. "Mary's shy around strangers." He gave her a smile as he said it. "She was looking forward to playing with your younger children."

"I believe they're all still napping," Miss Bennet said.

Mr. Taylor turned to her and Caroline could all but read the appreciation in his eyes as they settled on her fair visage. She pressed her lips into a thin line. Men didn't look at her that way. Nor would they ever, if she stayed in Miss Bennet's presence. Of course, that was good. She wanted Mr. Taylor to be appreciative of Miss Bennet's qualities. Surely she did.

If Mr. Taylor married Miss Bennet, Charles would be safe from her charms. If he married Miss Elizabeth, Caroline would no longer have her as a rival for Mr. Darcy's affections. Mr. Taylor attaching himself to either of the Bennet sisters could only increase Caroline's happiness.

Suddenly eager to be away from company and not wanting to interfere with Mrs. Gardiner's matchmaking, Caroline found herself saying, "I would be happy to entertain Mary in the nursery until the other children wake."

Mr. Taylor turned his smile on her. "Thank you. That would be most kind of you."

Caroline felt a strange flutter in her chest. She found herself smiling back.

"I'll show you the way," Mrs. Gardiner said.

She left the room, Mr. Taylor following her, Caroline a step behind. It wasn't until they started up the steps that she recalled she was still wearing Miss Elizabeth's unfashionable dress and that her lace was lopsided and coming loose. She felt her face heat, but there was no help for it now. Besides, it wasn't as if anyone important had seen her in this state. Mr. Darcy hadn't arrived yet, after all.

The nursery was a bright, pleasant room. It was decorated for Christmas, but the decorations were crafted of paper and paste, and obviously made by the children. Aside from the book and toy bedecked shelves that lined two walls, all of the furniture was child-sized. A thick carpet covered most of the floor.

"Any of the toys on these shelves are safe for young children," Mrs. Gardiner said, gesturing to the lower shelves of the bookcase. "Send for me if you require anything."

"Thank you," Caroline said.

Mrs. Gardiner nodded, leaving with a cheerful smile.

Caroline turned to Mr. Taylor. He set Mary on the floor, kneeling in front of her. "Miss Bingley is going to play with you, dear, until your cousins come in."

Mary leaned close, whispering something into his ear.

Mr. Taylor smiled, glancing at Caroline over the child's curls. "She looks like a very nice lady to me. I think it will be alright if you ask her to read to you."

"Of course it will be," Caroline said, unable not to answer his smile with one of her own. If he smiled at the Bennet sisters like that, one of them would surely be in love with him before the evening was out.

Mary turned to look up at her with wide blue eyes.

Caroline knelt, as her father had, and held out a hand. "Come, tell me what you would like me to read."

"I'll pick," Mary said, leaving her father to cross to the shelves.

"Are you sure you'll be all right with her?" Mr. Taylor asked, standing.

"Perfectly. If I'm not, I will call for help."

With a nod and another smile, Mr. Taylor left. Caroline sat on the floor, hoping Elizabeth's dress would get dirty. Mary returned from the shelves not with a book but clutching a pile of items that included a small doll and several wooden animals. They played with the toys for some time. Mary wasn't very talkative at first, but soon was happy to explain that the doll used to be Madeline's but she didn't play with it anymore, and the wooden farm animals were Ned's.

After they played for some time, Mary lifted those blue eyes to look at her. "We can read now."

"Yes, we can," Caroline agreed solemnly. "Do you want to pick?"

"Yes please." Mary went to an area of the shelves where the books were. While she looked through them, Caroline returned the doll and wooden animals to their original place.

Mary came over, holding up a book. "Read me Ned's book?"

Caroline sat down, quickly hiding her surprise when Mary climbed into her lap. Her arms about the child, she opened the book, flipping through. She frowned, seeing drawings so childish she couldn't believe anyone would put them in a book. Still, it was what Mary wanted to hear, and all of the books were likely childish. She turned to the beginning and read, "Ned's Book by Madeline Gardiner."

Caroline realized the book had been a blank book. While it was obvious an adult had written out the story, it was also obvious it was a story create by a child, with Miss Gardiner's childish pictures decorating every page. As she read it, Caroline was aware that it wasn't a badly drawn children's book, but an act of love by an older sister for her younger brother. She read the book to Mary twice, substituting Mary's name for Ned's.

Mary. Such a common name. Mr. Taylor, who was so handsome and dressed so well, had married into a family in trade and named his daughter unimaginatively. Caroline wondered how such a thing could have happened, but the thought struck her that it was Christmas and it was the wrong day to object to the name Mary.

They were about to begin the book for a third time when the Gardiner children came into the room. Mary climbed out of Caroline's lap and ran toward them. Caroline felt oddly deserted. She stood up, watching the children play and laugh, oblivious to her.

With a small smile for the ease of children, she went to change for dinner. She took off Miss Elizabeth's dress and regretted that it had not gotten dirty from sitting on the floor. She supposed Mrs. Gardiner's housekeeper was too good to permit that. She fixed her hair and redressed in her own gown, much finer than the borrowed one. When Miss Bingley finally descended the stairs to the drawing room, Mr. Darcy, Miss Darcy, Charles and Mr. Hurst were just arriving.

Mr. Darcy was his usual self, not smiling, not verbose and not a hair on his head out of order. Miss Bingley noticed his eyes went immediately to Miss Elizabeth, but before she had time to take exception to that she caught sight of Mr. Taylor's smile. That smile was turned on her. In fact, he was watching her and had been since she came into view. Miss Bingley felt the unacceptable urge to blush.

Dinner found her seated between Mr. Taylor and Miss Darcy, who looked a bit thinner and more pale than usual. Being seated beside Miss Darcy would normally have pleased Miss Bingley. She preferred every opportunity to further her cause with Mr. Darcy, and he was excessively swayed by his sister's opinion. Miss Darcy responded to her overtures in monosyllables as usual, though, and Miss Bingley found she didn't have her normal patience for it. Mary Taylor was a more satisfying conversationalist. The meal quickly turned into a series of long silences after each of Miss Bingley's attempts to engage Miss Darcy.

"Thank you for entertaining my daughter. I checked in on you a couple of times, but you both were so engrossed in what you were doing you didn't appear to see me," Mr. Taylor said on Caroline's other side.

She turned to him, gratified for the reprieve from trying to draw out Miss Darcy. "Mary is delightful. I enjoyed my time with her," she said. Oddly, it flickered through her head to wonder if it was Caroline or Miss Bingley who spoke.

"Do you have much experience with children?" he asked.

"Almost none." His eyes were blue as well, though a deeper shade than his daughters.

"You did remarkably well, then. She usually takes some time to get used to adults." He added a warm smile to his praise.

Miss Bingley was unsure what to say to that. His kind smile and approval flustered her, and she wasn't certain why. Why should she fight not to blush, when all he'd done was say she'd done well minding his child?

"Mr. Charles Bingley is your brother?" he asked her, nodding toward where Charles spoke quietly with Miss Bennet.

"Yes," Miss Bingley replied.

"Are you related to a Charles Bingley who died about two years ago? He made a fortune in canals."

"My father." Miss Bingley frowned slightly. She didn't care to be reminded of her father's connection to trade.

"My father and I did some business with him before he died. He was a good man."

Though she didn't wish to encourage a line of conversation based around trade, she was warmed by his regard for her father. "Thank you for saying so. I miss him." As she said it, she was struck by how true it was, especially on Christmas.

"I miss my father as well. He died a year and a half ago, just a month after my wife. It was almost too much grief for me to bear."

"I'm sorry," she said, not knowing what else to say to that. She had the strangest urge to place her hand atop his, where it rested on the table.

"Yes, well, thank you." He cleared his throat, looking away.

Caroline berated herself. How had she permitted the conversation to turn to such morbid things? It wasn't correct of her. No matter he'd led them in that direction. She traversed the upper echelons of society. Her conversational skills were a work of art. It was her duty not to permit such faux pas to transpire.

"What is it you do, Mr. Taylor? Do you work in canals?" Caroline didn't wish to speak of business, but she knew too little of him to come up with another topic in time to save the conversation. She didn't want him to dwell on grief. It was Christmas.

He turned back to her, looking relieved. "I do not, though I have several other interests. In fact, Mr. Gardiner and I are even now planning a joint venture with two other businessmen. We're buying a ship to trade with India." His eyes took on a slightly far off look, his obvious enthusiasm making him suddenly seem younger, hardly old enough to have two children and be a widower. He shook his head, his expression turning ruefully. "As it turns out, I disrupted the Gardiners' Christmas plans. I'm afraid I rush into things sometimes, when I become enthusiastic. I insisted we meet this week to finalize our venture. I didn't realize until Mrs. Gardiner gently hinted at it that they had other plans. Apparently, they were to visit Mr. Gardiner's sisters in Hertfordshire, but remained in town because of me." He cast a smile toward their host. "I apologized, but he assured me it is nicer to have his nieces visit, because they get along so well with his children."

Caroline privately thought there were other reasons to stay in London, rather than subject themselves to the Bennets and Phillips, but wouldn't dream of saying as much. For the rest of the first course, she chatted pleasantly with Mr. Taylor. Somehow, he brought back memories of her father, who would talk business until her mother would tell him not to encourage his children to think about trade. She missed hearing her father's passion for his work. She never would have believed it before.

Louisa always said they shouldn't be sorry he'd died, that it made it easier for them to move in the best circles, but what were the best circles? The Gardiners didn't qualify, yet she enjoyed being with them. She was having a more pleasant Christmas than she could recall enjoying for years. Would a stuffy affair at the Hursts with only them and the Darcys really have been better than spending the day with the Gardiners and Mr. Taylor?

She looked across the table at Mr. Darcy, realizing she'd hardly paid him a moment's attention, hardly even thought about him all day. He was talking to Elizabeth Bennet. Even from across the table, Caroline could see the intensity in his gaze when he regarded Miss Elizabeth. He spoke with more animation and passion than he'd ever used with Caroline.

The foolishness of her rivalry with Miss Elizabeth suddenly struck her. It wasn't a rivalry. Mr. Darcy was so clearly and completely taken with Miss Elizabeth, there was no room for a rival. He didn't care about Caroline. Not at all. She didn't know if he would stoop to marrying Miss Elizabeth, but it was obvious he cared more for her than he did for anyone else, with the possible exception of Georgiana.

Thinking of Miss Darcy reminded Caroline of her social obligations. Whether Mr. Darcy cared about her or not, Caroline was refined and would behave so. Neither she nor Georgiana were talking now, which couldn't be permitted at a dinner party. As the more experienced person, it was up to Caroline to rectify that.

"Miss Darcy," Caroline said. "Your brother is unhappy when you don't talk in company. Just follow my lead and we will fool him into thinking we are having an interesting conversation. A, B, C, D, E, F, G."

"What?"

"It's you turn. It doesn't have to be the alphabet. You can count. You can recite nursery rhymes or the words of songs."

Miss Darcy started with H and finished the alphabet. Then she frowned slightly. "I spoke more than you did."

"You did." Miss Bingley started on nursery rhymes. Miss Darcy added some of her own. They spoke very softly, to avoid having others hear what they were saying. It didn't really engage Miss Bingley's mind, leaving her to wonder that she was speaking nursery rhymes to an adult but didn't use them with a child. She was also able to observe her brother and Miss Bennet become more and more engaged in each other's conversation, but could think of little to do about it.

The evening went on in a similar fashion. There was pleasant conversation with Mr. Taylor one course, and inanities with Miss Darcy the next. No one was subtly spiteful. No one was evaluating her every gesture or critiquing her attire and manners. All in all, it was a very enjoyable Christmas.

When the time came to depart for the evening, Mr. Taylor appeared with her cloak, holding it out to help her into it.

Caroline knew she should protest such familiarity, but he was exceedingly handsome and had paid her every attention all evening. Not to mention, his eyes were such a lovely, deep blue and he spoke kindly about her father. So, she turned her back to him, permitting him to settle her cloak about her shoulders.

"That was a kind thing you did for Miss Darcy," he said in her ear, his hands lingering on her shoulders. "I've never met anyone quite like you, Miss Bingley. May I call on you?"

Caroline shivered, but this time the reaction had nothing to do with the cold. In fact, she could feel heat touching her cheeks. "Yes," she said softly. "I would like that."

Caroline Bingley left the Gardiners home with a smile. It had been a very nice Christmas indeed.

Epilogue

A year later, Caroline spent Christmas at Pemberley. It was as perfect as she'd dreamed it could be, but for different reasons than she'd imagined. Her only slight remorse was Louisa's absence. Her sister was too concerned about bringing her young son on so long a journey to visit Pemberley. Louisa spent little time with the fashionable world and instead she spent it with other young mothers, where they talked endlessly about their children. Caroline sometimes enjoyed that kind of talk, because she was now the mother of two children, but sometimes she wanted to be with adults talking about adult things.

She wouldn't permit her sister's limitations to hamper the joy of the season, Pemberley and good company. Caroline wasn't certain if she and Joseph had become friends of Mr. Darcy's, or if they were invited because her brother had married the former Jane Bennet, whose sister had married Mr. Darcy. It might have been because Caroline was now mother to Mrs. Gardiner's nieces, or even because Miss Darcy now genuinely liked her. The truth was, it didn't exactly matter, because she was among friends.

Not close friends. None of these people were her dearest companions. To her surprise, she'd found those among her husband's friends. Now, her place in life happily settled, she could enjoy the society she once strived for, even if she didn't really belong to it. She'd found all the belonging she needed in Joseph's love.

Caroline smiled at him, where he stood speaking with Mr. Darcy and Charles. She was content in her happiness and it was Christmas again. Christmas was always a wonderful time of year.

~ The End ~

Their Secret Love

Chapter One

After Trafalgar jumped the fence, Darcy pulled him back to a walk. He suspected the fence, a clear delineator, meant he no longer rode on the land belonging to the property Bingley was considering leasing. It made sense to look at neighboring lands, but Darcy preferred to do so at a slower pace. He didn't wish to inadvertently stumble onto a crop or even a rabbit hole.

Darcy felt relatively certain Bingley would lease the property, called Netherfield Park. Bingley had expressed pleasure with the principal rooms and the rest of the manor also seemed suitable and well maintained, as Darcy had discovered the grounds to be. It slightly amused him that he'd had to insist on looking at everything from the kitchen and the attics. Bingley hadn't thought about anything beyond the entrance hall, ballroom, dining room, and master suite.

The agent of the owner had permitted the two of them to occupy the manor for two days and nights. A wise move on his part, as the beds were comfortable, the bedrooms well furnished, and the country mornings invigorating. The staff served an excellent dinner. While that only ensured they could, not that they always would, it provided a high recommendation for the level of service they could deliver. A level they seemed likely to maintain, as Bingley wasn't required to keep them.

After riding for another quarter of an hour, Darcy had gone much farther abroad than the previous day. He brought Trafalgar to a halt atop a low hill and scanned the view. Lovely, if a bit wild. Not as familiar as Derbyshire. Not quite as appealing to his senses, but more than adequate. Certainly, the flora glowed a verdant green, even under a glowering sky, and wildlife flourished.

Looking about again, with less an eye for beauty and more of one for practicality, he realized the only way he could return to Netherfield Park was to retrace his steps. He'd taken many twists and turns on his ride, each change in direction dictated either by the terrain or whim. With the high, thick cloud cover, he couldn't use the sun for direction.

He whirled Trafalgar in a tight circle, then rode back down the hill. Heading back the way he'd come, he returned to a familiar fenced pasture and halted to get his bearings. The pasture stood out in his memory for being almost overgrazed. As he recalled and could easily see, the next field over had lush grass that the cows contentedly munched. Suddenly feeling the passage of time, Darcy pulled free his pocket watch, to find he'd been absent longer than was reasonable. Reexamining the sparse grass of the field, Darcy decided he could let Trafalgar canter without doing any harm.

He urged Trafalgar forward, gaining enough speed to jump the low fence. Darcy smiled, enjoying the sensation of sailing through the air on a sure steed. Trafalgar landed smoothly and leapt forward into his canter. He'd barely taken two strides when he stumbled and fell.

Darcy hurtled through the air, an altogether less pleasant sensation. He hit the ground, landing on his back with a whooshing thump. He struggled to suck air. Coughed, gasping. The world executed a dizzying swirl. He concentrated on getting breath back into his lungs.

Once he could breathe again, he carefully moved each limb. Finding nothing amiss, he reached up and felt the back of his head but located no particular area of hurt. He patted the ground, finding no rocks where his skull had crashed down. He drew in a long, deep breath. Nothing particularly pained him.

Slowly and carefully, Darcy rose to his feet. Everything appeared to be in working order, his limbs miraculously unharmed by the fall. Tentatively at first, but with more vigor when no pain shot through him, he dusted at his clothing. Trafalgar stood a short distance away, watching. Darcy's hat rested on the ground near his horse.

Cautiously, Darcy walked toward his horse. Trafalgar wasn't trying to graze. He didn't shy away or approach. Simply remained oddly still. Darcy reached him and, ignoring his hat, secured the reins.

"Sir, are you all right?"

Darcy whirled around to look at the owner of the voice. He would have done so with more decorum, but the five words were musical to his ears. Liquid melody. He'd never imagined a voice could be so lovely, and this despite being touched with concern.

As he turned to face her, he almost closed his eyes, but forced them to remain open. He steeled for disappointment. No one could be as beautiful as that melodic voice hinted.

Bright, dark eyes peered out of heavy lashes. A few strands of hair escaped, but they only enhanced the loveliest face he ever had seen. As she gracefully walked toward him, he saw her figure was as elegant and appealing as the rest of her.

He blinked to dispel the vision. Then again. Absently, he raised a hand to reexamine his head for injury. The vision before him didn't waver, only moved nearer.

"I'm unharmed," he managed to say. He wanted to say more but was afraid to shatter this dream. Surely, a creature this lovely had every intension of disappearing in a puff of smoke, to exist only in the depths of his imagination. In his dreams.

"Your horse isn't."

"Isn't what?" he asked, confused.

"Isn't unharmed." She issued an elegant gesture toward Trafalgar. "He was limping after he got up. Off fore."

Darcy stared at her a moment. An eyebrow winged up and he realized she expected something from him. He blinked, then turned to Trafalgar.

Stepping back, Darcy gave a gentle pull on the reins. Trafalgar, as loyal a steed as a man could ask, followed. Indeed, the right front leg was lame. Looping the reins over his arm, Darcy checked the leg. It didn't appear to be broken.

He turned to the woman. Panic shot through him. Her back to him, she walked away. A cry formed on his lips, but before the sound could issue forth, she dipped down and picked up something.

She turned back, holding out a horseshoe. "I saw this fly off, just before your horse fell." To Darcy's relief, she started back in his direction.

"Thank you," he said when she returned and proffered the shoe. He accepted it, then made to doff his hat, before realizing he'd yet to retrieve it. "My name is Darcy, by the way." He bowed.

"Elizabeth Bennet." She paused. For the first time, hesitation touched her expression. "Miss Elizabeth Bennet." She curtsied.

Elation shot through him. She wasn't married. And she wanted him to know that.

"Miss Bennet, I am in need of direction."

"Where to, sir?" A touch of challenge brightened her eyes, adding another layer of appeal. "And how is it you do not know the way? Is your destination different from whence you've ridden?"

A jolt of surprise followed her words. No one ever questioned him. "I came from Netherfield Park and I can find my way back by retracing my route, but I cannot have a lame horse jump a fence." He had jumped several on his way and he didn't remember if they all had gates. He decided to issue a challenge of his own. "Do you know the lay of the land well enough to direct me to a route that does not have fences?"

She paused for long enough to make him worry that she could not, before saying, "The shortest way requires crossing a stream." Her gaze dropped to his well-shined hessians before returning to his face, the glimmer of a dare lurking within her fine eyes. "The stream is not deep, but your boots will get wet."

His valet would be in fits, but Darcy kept his face neutral and replied, "Then they will get wet. I imagine I will survive the experience."

"A new one for you, sir?"

Did she tease him, this Miss Elizabeth Bennet? Always in the past, the distant past now, when anyone had teased him, usually his one-time friend George Wickham, Darcy had felt a sting of shame and anger. Now, a strange warmth spread through him. He almost enjoyed the challenge implicit in her words. "Not new, but not recent."

As if that reply satisfied her, her demeanor relaxed. "The way is too complicated to describe, but I can show you."

"Please. I would be very grateful." More grateful because of your company, Elizabeth, he thought. Even her name was enchanting.

She flashed a smile. "I'll retrieve your hat."

Elizabeth returned with his hat, the garment not much worse from flying from his head, then led the way across the field. They walked slowly at first, both watching Trafalgar intently, but his limp didn't get worse and he didn't resist being led. After a time, Darcy relaxed, less worried for his horse.

As if sensing his change in mood, the next time Elizabeth glanced away from their path it was to look up at Darcy askance, not to check his horse. "Might you satisfy my curiosity as to why you must reach Netherfield Park, Mr. Darcy?"

"My friend, Bingley, is considering leasing it. He asked me to come help him decide."

"He must either value your opinion highly or his own quite little."

Darcy suspected both, but as she gave him the choice of belittling Bingley or promoting himself, he remained silent. He rather suspected her words constituted another small test of character.

"Do you think he'll take it?" she asked after a time, leading him down a hill to a gate in the fence.

"Yes."

They crossed a well-trod path, then entered a narrower one that snaked into a grove of maples. To his relief, the path remained wide enough to walk side by side, Trafalgar trailing.

"Will you visit him, your friend who might lease Netherfield Park?"

Darcy's heart thudded. Did she wish him to? "If you are any example of the company to be found in Hertfordshire, I most certainly will." He regretted the words, so very forward, almost instantly. They sounded like something a charming man would say. Someone like Wickham. Whenever Darcy attempted charming, he failed.

"I daresay I am one example. I live about three miles from Netherfield Park, in Longbourn."

He tried to read her tone. To his ear, she didn't sound displeased.

"There is the stream," she said, pointing.

Disappointment filled him. Not because his boots would definitely get wet, but because he couldn't ask her to cross the wide, shallow swath of gurgling water. Her feet would become soaked, as would her hem, unless she held it up to a slightly indecorous height. That image filling his mind, his heart sped up once more.

"You should cross there," she said, pointing.

He turned to her and manfully suppressing his sorrow at her eminent departure, surprised at the depth of the feeling. Maybe he had hit his head after all? "Please, give me directions. You cannot cross."

Laughter bubbled from her, the sound like silver bells. She whirled and headed off, upstream. Darcy watched her disappear into the dense trees. Had she been a woodland spirit after all?

He shook his head. With no choices before him but forward or back, he led Trafalgar to the stream. His mount wanted to drink, so Darcy paused to let him. As Trafalgar raised his head, movement upstream caught Darcy's eye.

He turned to see Elizabeth, arms flung wide for balance, all but skipping across a fallen log. She reached the other side, flashed him a smile, and disappeared into the trees again. Darcy tugged on Trafalgar's reins.

Halfway across the stream, water sloshing to mid-shin height, Darcy almost tripped on a rock, his attention rivetted on where Elizabeth might reappear on the path ahead, rather than on his footing. As he and Trafalgar climbed from the streambed, she emerged on the path before them, his woodland sprite come to lead him onward. Darcy couldn't help but return her smile.

She glanced at Trafalgar. "I didn't mean to abandon you to the stream while I remain dry, but you could never have gotten him through the rocks and underbrush, with him lame. Besides, you couldn't have led your horse and balanced at the same time."

"You have me off balance."

She stared at him, smile lost as her lips formed an *O* of surprise.

Something akin to fear shot through him. He'd attempted charming again and, as always, he'd botched it. He'd scared her. Offended her. How could he make it right? He blurted, "Do you believe in love at first sight?"

She shook her head. "I do not. Attraction, yes. Not love."

"Well then, I'm attracted to you like I've never been attracted to another woman. I know nothing about you, but part of me wants to take you in my arms and never let you go." Surely, he was mad to say such things.

She backed up a step, in silent agreement to his thought, her eyes wide with worry.

Chapter Two

As a gesture of goodwill, Darcy took a step back as well, bumping into Trafalgar's nose. He couldn't let her leave. He might never find her again. "Do not misunderstand. I would never be so ungentlemanly as to act on the desire. I'm as stunned as you that I even admitted it aloud."

She eyed him, amusement and teasing buried by uncertainty and a touch of fear.

Darcy drew in a settling breath. He must stop sounding like a madman before Elizabeth ran away. Not only would he lose her, he and Trafalgar were themselves lost. He needed her. In too many ways. More ways and more deeply, and suddenly, than he'd ever deemed possible.

Trying again he said, "I want to court you. Please."

Wryness chased the shadow from her face. "Unless you are in debt, as soon as you make the slightest move toward me, my mother will announce to the world that you're going to marry me." She shook her head. "If you try to court me, my mother's behavior will embarrass me." She grimaced. "Actually, it will likely embarrass you as well and possibly hurt your reputation."

It shocked him to realize he would marry her in a heartbeat. Fear of pressure from her mother, of harm to his reputation, held no weight. He'd only suggested courtship because he feared the word marriage would cause her to flee.

"On top of that, she will insist I marry you," Elizabeth continued. "I mean no offense, but I would prefer the chance to come to know you and decide for myself before my mother attempts to force the union on me."

If her mother's help was what it would take, Darcy would tell the woman of his intentions today.

Or would he? Could he afford to behave so rashly? In the forest, the stream gurgling behind him, only he and the enchanting Miss Elizabeth existed, but that reality couldn't be his. Darcy had duties. Obligations. Most he would gladly toss aside for the vision before him, but one he could not.

"You appear doubtful." A wistful note touched Elizabeth's lovely voice, but her wry smile remained. "Even though you haven't met her, my mother already dooms our courtship before it is begun." She quirked a smile. "Or are you in debt, Mr. Darcy? Judging by your wardrobe and horseflesh, I might have guessed you overspend."

He shook his head. "It is not that. I have a sister."

Elizabeth tipped her head to the side. "And you've already ascertained she will not approve of me?"

"She will adore you." He felt as certain of that as of his love for this woman. Elizabeth Bennet was exactly the spark of light and vibrance both he and Georgiana needed in their lives.

Elizabeth's expression questioned. "Not that I wish to push this courtship on you, but you have piqued my curiosity, sir. How does your sister come between what is not yet even begun?"

It was begun, so far as Darcy was concerned. Begun and concluded. Now that he'd met Elizabeth, he could as much live without her as air. Tamping down that mad sounding declaration, he instead offered, "Both of our parents are deceased."

Sympathy welled in her eyes. "I am sorry to hear that, both for you and your sister."

"Thank you." His mother's death was an infrequently recalled memory, and after over four years, he often went days without thinking about his father, but hearing the genuine regret in Elizabeth's voice brought poignant pain. He cleared his throat to continue. "My sister, Georgiana, is the joint ward of myself and my cousin, Colonel Richard Fitzwilliam." How could he explain without revealing too much? He owed Georgiana secrecy.

"And?" Elizabeth prompted, curiosity alive on her face.

"Colonel Fitzwilliam is very likely to get a command." No, that wasn't where to begin.

"That will be good for him, I assume?"

Absently, Darcy nodded. "Yes, for him, but not for our joint guardianship of Georgiana." Trafalgar let out a huff, nudging Darcy as if encouraging him to continue. "My father was aware that Colonel Fitzwilliam might feel his military duties are more important than his guardianship. By my father's will, if Colonel Fitzwilliam leaves the country, he can either allow me to be sole guardian or pass his half of the responsibility along to his brother." He paused, seeking words both correct and diplomatic. He'd no call to slander his older cousin, the Earl of Matlock.

"And this would be bad?" Elizabeth prompted.

Darcy offered another nod, this one more emphatic. "Both Colonel Fitzwilliam and I agree that his brother would be a poor choice for a guardian. Not absolutely horrible, but he's already mentioned that he feels it's in Georgiana's best interest to marry quickly. He would have some authority." Elizabeth didn't need to know that authority was amplified by a title. She would suspect Darcy of trying to aggrandize himself. "He would use that authority to push a match on her. He also thinks her best match would be with someone significantly older."

Elizabeth's features crinkled slightly with confusion. "How do you know his thoughts on this so well? Can you be certain of them?"

Darcy assayed a slight smile. "Colonel Fitzwilliam's older brother is not…subtle. He's accustomed to being obeyed and has many opinions, with which he is very free. He became guardian of his sister when she was fourteen and arranged a marriage for her when she was barely sixteen. He's already attempted to cow Colonel Fitzwilliam into arranging a similar marriage for Georgiana."

"Perhaps your sister is lucky to have so many people concerned for her wellbeing. Does she wish to wed for wealth or position?"

A grimace he couldn't contain crossed Darcy's face. She'd wished to wed George Wickham, for a brief, insane time. Until Darcy had shown up and thwarted what was an obvious attempt on Wickham's part to secure Georgiana's dowry. Something for which Darcy would never forgive his one-time friend. "My sister is only fifteen and too young for marriage. She is also painfully reserved." Which was why she needed Elizabeth in her life. "Even if Georgiana resisted a marriage that wasn't her choice, it would be difficult for her." She was too persuadable, which was why Wickham had almost succeeded in eloping with her.

Elizabeth frowned slightly, brow marred by a single line as she thought. "If your cousin, this Colonel Fitzwilliam, knows his brother's inclinations and has already staved them off, why would he pass on his half of your sister's guardianship to the man?"

Darcy dropped his gaze to the leaf dotted path. "I made a poor choice for my sister's governess. A horrible choice. Nearly disastrous. Colonel Fitzwilliam mistrusts my judgment because of that. He's content with the status quo as long as he's in the country and I consult him on my decisions, but if he goes to the continent, to war, he cannot monitor my choices." Darcy worked not to clench his teeth. "My actions on Georgiana's behalf prior to the incident have been worthy, and since, impeccable. I feel I've nearly recaptured Colonel Fitzwilliam's good opinion."

About them, leaves rustled. Darcy wondered how long they'd stood thus, by the stream. It didn't matter. Let Bingley wait. Let him mount a search. Darcy would remain in Elizabeth's company for so long as he might.

He looked back up at her, stunned anew by her perfection. "I would not care if your mother insists we wed immediately. I'd procure the special license myself. But I cannot afford to appear rash. I require my cousin's good opinion so that, when he takes his new commission, he'll turn over his half of Georgiana's guardianship to me." Hope flashed through Darcy at a new thought. "Do you happen to be an heiress or of noble descent? If you are either, Colonel Fitzwilliam and his brother might both forgive a hasty marriage." And if Elizabeth hadn't any dowry or connections, even an unhasty courtship of her might make his relations consider him unfit as a guardian for Georgiana.

A frown touched her lovely face. "My father is a gentleman, but the estate is entailed away. I doubt he could muster five hundred pounds for my dowry. I have relatives in trade."

"That is unfortunate," Darcy said. She took another step backward. He had to make himself clear or she might leave. "Not that it matters to me," he said in haste. "But because it means we will have to wait until Colonel Fitzwilliam leaves the country before I may court you. With your background, we can't let a ghost of a suspicion escape. No word of my courting you can be allowed to reach my relations."

"But all this would change if I had a large dowry?" Her tone conveyed censure. "Is money so important to you, Mr. Darcy?"

He shook his head. "I won't even ask for a dowry." Not if he could have Elizabeth. "And my relatives would deem me crazy for that."

Elizabeth's expression grew contemplative. "I see," she said slowly. The line of thought cleared from her brow. "You are afraid that if you behave in a way that appears rash, such as meeting a woman in a pasture and wedding her before the week is out, your cousin Colonel Fitzwilliam will have fresh conviction that you are an unfit sole guardian for a fifteen year old girl. I can even understand that he might believe you being willing to wed a woman with relatives in trade and with no dowry shows that you do not have the appropriate values to monitor your sister."

Despite the dire nature of their discussion, Darcy's mood lightened. How rare to find anyone who understood him so well. Usually, he blundered through conversations, alienating rather than pleasing. Unless with close friends, he'd taken to saying as little as possible, to avoid the consequences of his inevitable errors.

"Your cousin would be right."

Darcy's moment of pleasure fled at her words. "I am a good guardian to my sister."

Elizabeth offered a smile. "I do not doubt that, sir, but your interest in me shows that you do not share your cousin's values. Even if you needn't require a bride to bring money or connections, it would be rash to propose to a woman you've only just met."

"Yet I feel that if I don't do so I will regret it for the rest of my life."

She shook her head. "Perhaps. But you might regret it more if we married. We don't know each other." Her lips quirked. "I could be a terrible hoyden."

Darcy had always thought he was a rational, logical person. Now he realized he wasn't. Any outsider would agree with Elizabeth's argument. What was it about her that made him lose his reason? "Perhaps your presence destroys my sense, but I do want to propose to you."

She held up a staying hand. "I would be lying if I said you do not intrigue me, sir. Another lie would be to say that intrigue doesn't run deeper than any I've felt before, but you will betray a disturbing level of madness if you propose to me, here and now, having known me little more than an hour."

Darcy swallowed down the words. Instead, he managed, "You are correct, of course. I should come to know you better. Then we can see."

A fresh smile turned up her lips. "I would like that."

"To more fully answer an earlier question of yours, Bingley has invited me to stay with him if he takes possession of the lease. I refused, but I can change my mind."

"Then what?" she asked, her tone encouraging, giving him hope. "We may have solved your problem of appearing rash to your cousin, but we would still have my overzealous mama with whom to contend, along with my relations in trade and my lack of a dowry."

He shook his head. He didn't wish any more obstacles. "We can meet in the normal course of events."

"And let my mother read the look I even now see in your eyes?" Her cheeks reddened with the words, her blush beguiling. "We'll be in the same predicament as if you meet her now."

His mind roiled. There must be a way. Not that he believed

Elizabeth's mother could be quite so formidable, but she obviously believed it. She wanted a solution. How would it appear if he could not muster one?

"We dislike each other," he declared. "Or at least pretend to. That should stop the rumors."

"But if we dislike each other, how can we come to know each other better?"

He frowned. How indeed?

"We could meet in secret," she suggested in a low voice, her cheeks recoloring. "I…it's a scandalous suggestion, I know, but we've already stood here alone together for longer than is proper. The line is crossed. Could it be so wrong to speak here again?"

Darcy looked about at the dense woodland. He could imagine few things more perfect than meeting his woodland sprite in this place. Eagerly, he asked, "When? How often?"

"Weekly? Wednesdays, perhaps, near dawn?" She studied his face with what he liked to hope was eagerness. "Do you rise early? I generally do."

He nodded.

"How will I know when our first meeting is to take place?" she asked. "You said your friend, this Mr. Bingley, hasn't even decided if he will take Netherfield Park."

"I have decided he will. I will meet you here, three weeks from today. It is unlikely I will arrive in Netherfield Park earlier."

"Three weeks from today, at dawn."

He nodded, an ache already forming at the idea of not seeing her again until then.

"It is important we not be seen together now, then," Elizabeth said.

She proceeded to give him the remainder of the directions to Netherfield Park. They were, as she'd intimated, complex, but Darcy felt up to the task. Any words uttered by Elizabeth were indelibly branded in his mind, even ones so mundane as directions. When she ceased speaking, they stood for a long moment, studying each other.

Finally, Elizabeth offered a dazzling smile. "I shall see you when you return to Hertfordshire, my mysterious Mr. Darcy. Wednesday. At dawn. If you see me before then, I hope you shall give me reason to pretend dislike."

Still smiling, she whirled and disappeared into the trees. Another long moment passed before Trafalgar nosed him again. With a light tug of the reins, Darcy led his horse away. Though he didn't believe in fairies or goblins, he hoped Elizabeth Bennet wasn't simply a dream. One he knew would never fade.

Chapter Three

Three weeks later, Elizabeth sneaked out at dawn. There was a drizzle, but it didn't deter her. She felt a giddy anticipation, and greatly daring. She arrived in the still shadowy grove early, hoping Mr. Darcy would be early too. He wasn't there.

Elizabeth paced beside the stream, anticipation warming her more than any crackling blaze or hot summer day ever could. She didn't own a watch but could observe the lessening of shadow under the trees. In time, long arms of pink morning light stretched across the ground, angling between the trees. The light turned yellow as the sun rose. Elizabeth waited. The hour grew so late, she knew she'd be questioned when she returned home, unable to now sneak back in unobserved.

Mr. Darcy never appeared. He'd lied. He likely hadn't ever intended to meet her. If he remembered her at all, he was probably smirking at the thought of the poor, naïve girl waiting for him alone in the woods.

Elizabeth returned home, offering a mumbled explanation about being unable to sleep, which was true so far as it went. She set about forgetting the incident. She went through her days as she always had but something, some level of happiness, eluded her. The clouds lifted and the sun returned, but the sky seemed less blue than before. The air held more chill, even when she walked with vigor. Nothing tasted as it should. Not even her favorite treats.

After a second week, she decided her strange dissatisfaction wouldn't last. True, she'd never been so intrigued by a gentleman before, but she knew nothing of this mysterious Mr. Darcy. Not even if Darcy was a real name. It was ridiculous to think she could be in love with the man. No man had ever captured her heart, and the first to do so would not be some stranger she'd met in a field.

Unfortunately, the further passage of time revealed that her decision not to languish affected her heart very little. The organ persisted in a dull ache that spread through her body to influence all things. If, indeed, she suffered from some sort of love, Elizabeth decided she cared little for the emotion. She began to feel that, in fact, she might be ill. Not enamored at all, but under the thrall of some sort of sickness brought on by traipsing through the forest in the chill morning air.

A low anger began to simmer in her. For permitting her heart to become engaged. For believing a complete stranger. For the trick he'd played on her, though to what end she'd no idea. Most likely, merely for amusement.

To add to Elizabeth's discomfiture, no rumor of anyone renting Netherfield Park passed her ears. There had been mention of two men spending two nights at Netherfield Park and not renting it. People were only mildly curious about that. This had happened several times in the past, and nothing ever came of it. People decided these latest two had simply wanted a place to stay for two nights without paying.

Elizabeth tried not to hold onto any hope, for there could be none. Her mother would have heard any rumor about a lease being signed and passed it along. Mrs. Bennet was nothing if not a gossip. Yet no such news came, and Elizabeth's days stretched on.

In hope of dispelling her malaise, she went to the meeting place again while on an afternoon walk. As she strode into the forest, she mused that she couldn't really call it a meeting place, because they didn't meet there. Reaching the stream, she looked around. It was a pleasant place. Why did her heart ache when she saw the light filtering through the trees, throwing dappled shade on the ground? Even the trunks were painted in… what was that? Something was wedged in a fork in a tree. She walked over and pulled it out. It was an oilskin package, carefully wrapped around a note.

>*To the one with the hat and the horseshoe,*
>*I am deeply sorry. I have been unavoidably detained. I will try to meet you seven weeks after the original meeting.*
>*There has been no change in the attitude of the person who lost both.*

She clutched the letter to her. Never had so short a letter given her so much pleasure. It also assured her of Mr. Darcy's intellect, for she noticed several things. How he said he still loved her without revealing it to any casual reader. How the note gave little information. At the most, someone might remember that Mr. Darcy's horse had lost a shoe, but that was unlikely. A lost shoe was too common an occurrence to be remarked upon. Even the genders were obscured. The message neither revealed anyone's identity nor hinted at what had happened. Every precaution had been taken to impart vital information to her, while doing no harm should the message fall into other hands.

But it hadn't fallen into other hands. Elizabeth's held it. Clutched it, in fact. Unable not to smile, she kept clutching it as she hurried home, her day suddenly brighter. Only by force of will did she manage to go about the remainder of it behaving as normal. Time seemed both sped up and slowed, but finally the day wound down and they all sat to dinner.

"My dear Mr. Bennet," Elizabeth's mother said from her place at one end of the table. "Have you heard? Netherfield Park is let at last."

Elizabeth suppressed a smile, then a swirl of doubt. Were her mother's words confirmation? She had to find out who'd let Netherfield Park. It could be the wrong person. She wondered if Mr. Darcy would meet her even if someone else let Netherfield Park. No. That was too much to ask. Yet, he'd seemed so sincere, so focused.

Mr. Bennet spared his wife a glance. "No. I had not."

"But it is," Mrs. Bennet asserted. She launched into a babble of conversation. Elizabeth listened intently, yet hardly able to focus, waiting, anticipating… "Bingley," Mrs. Bennet declared loudly.

That single word set Elizabeth's heart skipping about. She swallowed rapidly. Bingley. The name Mr. Darcy had used. His friend who would let Netherfield Park. It had happened at last.

"He came down on Monday in a chaise and four to see the place," her mother was saying when Elizabeth managed to focus once more on her words. "Apparently, he was here before with a friend of his. They didn't sign the lease then because there were some negotiations. The owner wanted more money than he'd originally told Mr. Bingley, but Mr. Bingley stood firm. Did you know about that?"

"While you flatter me with your supposition of my omniscience, I cannot say that I did, my dear."

"Harrumph," Mrs. Bennet muttered, suspicion on her face, before embarking on a rant about Mr. Bingley's eligibility.

Elizabeth floated through the next few days, earning odd looks from her older sister, Jane, though none of her other sisters seemed to notice. Elizabeth didn't care if Jane found her behavior odd. Soon, she would see Mr. Darcy again.

But Mr. Darcy did not appear. Elizabeth realized none of her mother's rumors spoke of guests. Yet it hadn't been seven weeks yet. Mr. Bingley did appear, being called on by Mr. Bennet and calling in return. Then Mr. Bingley vanished again as well, back to London.

Elizabeth knew not what to think. She attempted normal behavior. She even offered to help her youngest sister, Lydia, modify the gown she wished to wear to the upcoming assembly in Meryton. Though the stitching occupied Elizabeth's hands, it did little to ease her mind.

Then, joyously, more rumor surfaced. Their mother returned from calling on her friend, Lady Lucas, with news that Mr. Bingley had merely popped off to London to bring back more guests. Rumor had as many as twelve ladies and seven gentlemen returning to Hertfordshire with Mr. Bingley. Elizabeth didn't care about the exact numbers, so long as one of them turned out to be Mr. Darcy. She returned to readying for the assembly with renewed vigor.

But what if he wasn't as handsome as she recalled? Worse, what if she wasn't as beguiling to him as he'd first thought? The more she thought on his friend Mr. Bingley being able to afford Netherfield Park, and on how fine Mr. Darcy's attire and mount had been, the more she worried he would despair at her lack of connections and dowry. He'd said he didn't care a whit about them, that only his family would, but had that been a half-truth? A safeguard for him to hide behind?

Elizabeth cast a glance about the parlor in which she sat, stitching a disgracefully low neckline for Lydia's dress. Lydia, whom Elizabeth privately thought too young to be out, at fifteen, would surely embarrass them all at the assembly. And where Lydia led, Kitty wouldn't be far behind, despite being Lydia's senior. Mary, Elizabeth's middle sister, likely would behave well and go unnoticed, so long as she didn't sing, but Mrs. Bennet would fawn over Mr. Bingley and his guests. Elizabeth could count on her father to behave with normality and decorum, and for her sister Jane to be perfect and lovely. Given how silly her mother, Kitty and Lydia could be, that proved scant comfort.

Elizabeth worried at her lower lip as she stitched, nervousness renewed. It was one thing for Mr. Darcy to be enchanted by her, alone. Another to maintain that attraction in the face of meeting her family. Maybe he would be impressed enough by her father and Jane to ignore the rest. Jane, in particular, would impress anyone.

A flash of jealousy surged through Elizabeth, alien and unwanted. Jane was so pretty. So biddable. No man had ever noticed Elizabeth with Jane in the room. Mr. Darcy, obviously easily swayed to infatuation, hadn't seen Jane when he declared his affection for Elizabeth. When they all met at the assembly, assuming he was even among Mr. Bingley's guests, Mr. Darcy would set eyes on Elizabeth's older sister and know what true beauty was.

At the end of the lowered neckline on Lydia's gown, Elizabeth used her teeth to cut the thread. She drew her shoulders back. If Mr. Darcy wanted Jane once he saw her, let him court Jane. Elizabeth had no use for a gentleman who fell easily in and out of love.

Sorrow touched her resolve. She felt as if she'd lost Mr. Darcy already. How could a man who claimed to fall in love with her at a glance not fall easily in and out of love?

Chapter Four

Excitement, dread and resolve mingled in Elizabeth as they joined the assembly, the festivities well underway. Fully resolved to appear as normal, she molded a smile to her lips. A look about the room and an ear to the general gossip quickly told her no one from Netherfield Park, or anywhere outside the local area, yet attended.

When Mr. Bingley arrived, his company did not include twelve ladies and seven gentlemen, but only himself, two fine and important looking women and two other gentlemen. One of these Elizabeth did not know. The other, where her gaze fixed, was Mr. Darcy.

He wasn't as handsome as she recalled. He was more so. Dressed for evening with dark perfection. Upright. Broad of shoulder. Austere. His only flaw, that none of the warmth of that day in the forest touched his features.

He remained at the back of the room as the rest of his party moved forward. Taller than most, he scanned the crowd. His gaze collided with hers. Elizabeth parted her lips slightly, ready to smile. With no hint of recognition, his attention moved on. Mr. Bingley waved to the Lucases and crossed to greet them.

"The Lucases are artful people," Mrs. Bennet said. "They put themselves in position so that Mr. Bingley would greet them first."

Elizabeth didn't reply to that comment, nursing hurt over Mr. Darcy's lack of recognition, but she didn't believe the Lucas' location unduly artful. Mr. Bingley had turned right upon entering the room. If he had turned left, he would have met the Bennets, who were positioned to greet any visitor who came that way.

As the next set formed, Elizabeth saw Mr. Bingley lead her friend, Charlotte Lucas, to the floor. Mr. Darcy caught up to his party and offered his arm to one of the two elegant women with whom he'd entered. The way the woman, who stood rather tall, smiled at Mr. Darcy made it obvious she cared for him. What remained uncertain was if he reciprocated the feeling.

"Miss Elizabeth, will you dance with me?"

She turned to see one of her neighbors. While she'd rather dance with Mr. Darcy, at least now she wouldn't stand out, looking undesirable. Not that she ever wanted for partners, but there were more women in attendance than men, so at some point they must all sit out.

"I'd be pleased to," she replied and accepted his arm.

He led them to a spot far from the company from Netherfield Park. Elizabeth didn't know if she was upset or relieved that the intricacies of the dance would bring her near Mr. Darcy but once. She manufactured a smile and forced herself to give her partner the attention he deserved.

Toward the end of the dance, she passed Mr. Darcy. She hardly heard as he whispered, "I'm sorry." The steps of the dance took her back away.

Elizabeth fought against a change in expression. He was sorry? What did that mean? Did he regret the missed meeting? Did he no longer esteem her and apologized for that?

Mr. Darcy danced next with the other woman from his party. Elizabeth had a partner, but never drew near enough to Mr. Darcy to attempt speech. After that, he didn't dance with anyone else, while she had partners for the next two sets. When she wasn't asked for the fifth, Elizabeth started to wend her way around the room in his direction. She knew they weren't to appear friendly, but they could at least be introduced and exchange a few words.

Charlotte Lucas, Elizabeth's particular friend, appeared beside her. "Are you feeling well?"

"Yes, perfectly well." Only, she wasn't. She longed to speak with Mr. Darcy.

"You seem distracted. Usually, all you have to do is smile and a partner appears," Charlotte said.

Elizabeth smiled at her friend. "I'm not sad or sick. I'm just in an odd mood." She had to be partially honest with her friend, both out of friendship and practicality. Charlotte was intelligent and observant. She would not believe there was nothing wrong with Elizabeth.

"Smile at the men, not me," Charlotte said.

Elizabeth made a face and Charlotte laughed, as Elizabeth intended her to do. She considered mentioning that she should smile at Lydia's lowcut gown, but she couldn't enjoy being embarrassed by her sister when Mr. Darcy was in the room. Somehow, Lydia's behavior seemed less amusing with him around.

Effectively halted from approaching Mr. Darcy by Charlotte's presence, Elizabeth forced herself to listen as Charlotte spoke about her conversation with Mr. Bingley, all the while hoping Mr. Darcy would come over. He didn't. Disappointment swirled through her. Yet...she'd told him they must pretend not to know one another, and he'd told her how important it was he not appear impulsive.

"That one thinks a lot of himself, does he not?" Charlotte asked at Elizabeth's side.

"Who?" Elizabeth blinked rapidly, attempting to orient her thoughts.

"That fine gentleman who came in with Mr. Bingley and remains at the back of the room, as if we're all too sordid to mingle with."

"Oh, yes, him."

Charlotte cast her a quick glance. Elizabeth mustered a mischievous look. Charlotte knew her too well. She would come to ready conclusions should Elizabeth permit her true emotions to show.

"Oh dear. It's almost as if he heard me," Charlotte whispered. "He's coming this way."

Elizabeth turned to see Mr. Darcy approaching. Hope rose in her, but he didn't look at her. Out of the corner of her eye, she noted Mr. Bingley cutting through the crowd, angled to meet Mr. Darcy. When they converged, Mr. Darcy halted with his back to her, his stance stiff and unyielding, a sharp contrast to Mr. Bingley's affable visage, flushed from dancing.

"Come, Darcy," said he, "I must have you dance. I hate to see you standing about by yourself in this stupid manner. You had much better dance."

Elizabeth didn't mean to overhear, but she could hardly help doing so. She covered her mouth to contain a giggle, for even though she believed Mr. Darcy to be less stiff than he pretended, she didn't deem him a man who enjoyed being called stupid.

"I certainly shall not. You know how I detest it, unless I am particularly acquainted with my partner. At such an assembly as this, it would be insupportable. Your sisters are engaged, and there is not another woman in the room whom it would not be a punishment to me to stand up with."

Charlotte elbowed Elizabeth, who turned to see her friend's eyes glinted with amusement.

"I would not be so fastidious as you are," cried Bingley, "for a kingdom! Upon my honor I never met with so many pleasant girls in my life, as I have this evening; and there are several of them, you see, uncommonly pretty."

Elizabeth and Charlotte exchanged a cheerful look, to hear themselves and their acquaintances described so.

"You are dancing with the only handsome girl in the room," said Mr. Darcy, looking at Jane.

Elizabeth pulled her gaze from Charlotte's before her friend could read the hurt and worry Mr. Darcy's comment stirred. She drew in a deep breath. It was not, after all, as if she didn't know Jane possessed the greater beauty. The pain came because, for the first time, Elizabeth cared.

Mr. Bingley turned to watch Jane as well. "Oh! she is the most beautiful creature I ever beheld! But there is one of her sisters just behind you, who is very pretty, and I dare say very agreeable. Do let me ask my partner to introduce you."

"Which do you mean?" and turning round, he looked for a moment at Elizabeth, till catching her eye, he withdrew his own and coldly said, "She is tolerable; but not handsome enough to tempt me; and I am in no humor at present to give consequence to young ladies who are slighted by other men. You had better return to your partner and enjoy her smiles, for you are wasting your time with me."

Mr. Bingley offered Elizabeth an apologetic grimace, then pivoted and walked away. Without a glance in her direction, Mr. Darcy stalked off. Elizabeth remained, mouth slightly open, eyes round, and pain tearing at her insides.

"How could he?" Charlotte placed a concerned hand on Elizabeth's arm. "The brute. No income in the world could justify such behavior. Lizzy, are you well?"

Elizabeth schooled her features into a wry smile, the process difficult with misery wringing through her, and turned to Charlotte. "Don't worry, Charlotte. I am in no humor to give consequence to the words of a supercilious gentleman whose behavior labels him the worst sort of snob."

Relief touched Charlotte's smile. "Unfortunately, his income is reputed to be as high as his pride. No woman here will refuse to dance with him, despite his bad behavior."

"His income?"

"Rumor has it that he has ten thousand pounds a year," Charlotte said.

"Ten thousand a year." Disappointment flowed through Elizabeth.

There was no way that such a man would be interested in her. Perhaps his insult was designed to impart as much.

Or did he mean to estrange them, as they'd discussed? She tried to tamp down hope, but that could be the impetus. If so, she should help by spreading the tale of his ill manners. If not, he deserved to have it spread for being so ill mannered. Elizabeth only wished, as she and Charlotte repeated the incident with much amusement, that she knew which.

Then Mr. Bingley asked her to dance. Elizabeth gladly accepted, hoping to learn more about Mr. Darcy, and soon realized Mr. Bingley's motive for partnering her; pity. He'd guessed she'd overheard Mr. Darcy's hateful comment and danced with her to console her. Elizabeth did not mind. Mr. Bingley danced well, and she still might learn something more of the mysterious, mercurial Mr. Darcy.

What was it in *Aesop's Fables*? A man is known by the company he keeps. Well, she found Mr. Bingley pleasant enough. He had good manners and he'd shown a genuine kindness in dancing with her immediately after Mr. Darcy's insult. Maybe she could permit some hope for Mr. Darcy after all.

Chapter Five

The following morning was to be their meeting. Elizabeth slipped out of bed before dawn, careful not to wake Jane, with whom she shared a room. Sleep had eluded Elizabeth for much of the night. She'd lain awake, attempting to sort out her feelings, unsure if she should even go to meet Mr. Darcy.

But she had to know. Which was the real Mr. Darcy? On the one hand, he played the snob so very well, and observation showed that Mr. Bingley's sisters echoed the sentiment. On the other, Mr. Bingley was Mr. Darcy's friend, not the man's sisters, and Mr. Bingley appeared all affability and kindness.

Elizabeth scooped up her garments and sneaked from the room, daring to dress in the hall so as not to disturb her sister. She left her hair braided and tiptoed downstairs. Mostly by feel, for Longbourn remained unlit and the sun a mere thought on the horizon, she donned boots, hat, gloves and cloak against the cool autumn air, then slipped out into the cusp of a new day.

Without seemed brighter, false dawn and the moon low on the western horizon, offering enough light to navigate the familiar trail she trod. She hoped Mr. Darcy would have similar luck. He'd farther to go and less experience with the land.

If he turned up.

She pushed away that thought and hurried her stride.

She reached the forest as the sun emerged in a blaze of orange and slipped into the concealing trees. Excitement at the prospect of seeing Mr. Darcy, at the sheer impropriety of her behavior, thrummed through her. It became a struggle to keep a safe pace on the shadowy, precarious forest path, her whole body ready to race forward.

A tall shadow waited in the center of the path by the stream. Elizabeth slowed, shyness washing over her. They'd met but the once. What if he really was the brute he'd seemed at the assembly? What if he no longer esteemed her? Squaring her shoulders, she marched forward.

"Elizabeth," he breathed, reaching out a hand.

She placed hers in it and he kissed the back of her glove, a mere token of affection through the kidskin. A delicious shiver ran up her arm, toward her heart. "Mr. Darcy. I did not know if you would come."

"Nothing could have kept me."

"Oh? Such vehemence for a woman who is not handsome enough to tempt you?" She tried to make her tone light, but the insult still stung.

"You said to give you an excuse to dislike me."

A smile sprang to her lips. The insult had been to fulfil her request, as she'd dared to hope. "You didn't give me an excuse, but a reason, sir."

"A reason?" Worry caught at his tone. The sun inched higher. Gold tinted light began to stretch through the leafless trees.

"I worried you were warning me that you didn't care for me anymore." She blushed at how forward she was. "You even said you were sorry."

He caught her other hand. Holding both, he tugged her near.

A tingling of alarm, mixed with excitement, shot through her. "Mr. Darcy, I—"

"No." He shook his head. "Do not worry. I will not dishonor you." He kept her hands but loosened his hold. "But were I to do so, I should take you in my arms and kiss away your every doubt."

Elizabeth's breath caught. In fear or excitement, she knew not which. Experimentally, she withdrew one hand. When he put no pressure on her other, made no move to retrieve the one she'd removed, she returned her fingers to his. Even through gloves, it felt right to hold him. "At the assembly, why did you say you were sorry?"

"Because I could not dance with you."

Elizabeth released a relieved breath. She hadn't enjoyed worrying. "That's very kind, but your apology made no sense to me, and made me fear it was for greater things."

"I did not mean to perturb you." He offered a rueful smile. "It didn't occur to me that you would doubt me."

Charlotte was correct. Mr. Darcy did think highly of himself. "How could I not? You weren't here when we planned. How could I not wonder?"

"Did you not get my note?" he asked, sounding a touch alarmed.

"Yes, but it said very little."

"I wanted you to know I care and meant to return, but I couldn't risk your reputation."

She wondered if that was the only reason. By leaving out all trace of who wrote or to whom, Mr. Darcy also protected himself. "You succeeded in that, but I still don't know what happened."

"First, the negotiations for Bingley's leasing Netherfield Park broke down when the owner wanted more money. Before that was solved, Georgiana's governess became quite ill. I arranged for Georgiana to live with me. She needed both a chaperone and to be removed from the source of infection." He shook his head. "I couldn't write you."

"Indeed not." Writing her would only be proper if they were engaged, which they were not, nor would be, until she came to know him better. "For how long will we pretend dislike while secretly coming to know one another, sir? Is there news on your cousin's deployment?"

"Everything is moving slower than it should. Colonel Fitzwilliam said that is normal, but I'm impatient and must conceal it. He was told he would leave in just over three weeks, but he thinks it will be double that. He's already written a document ceding full guardianship but won't sign it until the night before they ship out."

"Six weeks." In some ways, an eternity, but likely for the best. Elizabeth hadn't completely jested when she told Mr. Darcy she might be a hoyden. She was, a bit. She walked alone, spoke her mind, dreamed of marrying only where her heart was engaged, but she'd never felt so daring and rash as when she stood in the forest with this man. Six weeks would be a test of this impetuous affection they felt.

At least, that's what her mind told her, rational and calm. Pounding in her chest, her heart held very different ideas. Enough sunlight filtered through the trees now to illuminate Mr. Darcy's face. His strong features. The glow in eyes that studied her, wrenching at her resolve.

She pulled her hands free but offered a smile to reduce the sting. Wrapping her arms about her, she took a half step back, to bolster her resolve. "We are meant to come to know each other better."

Mr. Darcy let his arms fall to his sides. "What do you wish to know?"

"First, why were you quite so cruel at the assembly? Your insult stung, as did your comparison of me to my sister." She'd always thought Jane was prettier but didn't think a man who loved her would prefer Jane.

A long moment ticked by. Elizabeth could almost hear him going back over their conversation. Finally, a slightly startled look crossed his features, followed once more by thought.

"I thought you would understand that my insult was pretense. I was obviously wrong. The fault was mine, not yours." He stepped back slightly and bowed. "Miss Bennet," he said slowly, as if feeling out each word. "I apologize for my unwarranted and completely inaccurate insult. Your beauty outshone every other woman in attendance. You do tempt me, in every way. I wanted to follow you about the room, but knew if I came near you, you would draw me to you like a magnet. It took every ounce of strength not to go to you, to ask you to accompany me not for one set, but for every dance."

Elizabeth's eyebrows shot up. "I daresay a more thorough and flattering apology has never been uttered."

"Good." He moved nearer again. "Then you accept my apology?"

"I feel I must."

A smile curved his mouth. "Do we know each other better yet?"

Elizabeth yanked her gaze back up to his eyes. "Better, to be certain. Now tell me, sir, do you believe the task well enough done? May we behave more normally now, with our dislike firmly established?"

He shook his head. "It depends on how you view normality, for my version of it altered the moment I met you."

"How so?" she asked, quite intrigued.

"The pieces of my life lifted, swirled, and fell back to earth in a new order." He looked down appearing almost...embarrassed.

"Mr. Darcy, sometimes you seem deliberately obtuse."

"My behavior at the assembly was only a bit worse than customary. Certainly, insulting you was out of character, but refusing to dance was not. I've never before seen dancing as anything more than obligation. I hadn't understood the reason for it."

"Surely, your cousin will not deem a few dances make you into a bon vivant?"

"I cannot risk him hearing of a change in my ways until he signs."

She shook her head, beginning to wonder if Mr. Darcy thought he might take her for a fool. "How would he even hear?"

"Mr. Hurst." When she looked blank, he clarified, "The other man visiting Mr. Bingley."

As he spoke, Elizabeth realized she'd heard the name at the assembly, but promptly forgotten it. Mr. Darcy's employment of it did nothing to allay her suspicion. "That requires elaboration, sir."

"Mr. Hurst's sister is married to one of Colonel Fitzwilliam's cousins. They all gossip incessantly. I am fairly certain Mr. Hurst unofficially reports on me through his sister, to Colonel Fitzwilliam's cousin, and onward to Colonel Fitzwilliam."

"Fairly certain?"

"I cannot take the chance. Not when it is for such a short time. Georgiana's future is at stake."

Elizabeth would need to meet this vaunted sister of Mr. Darcy's. Were his words truthful, Miss Georgiana Darcy was a very fortunate young woman to have so loving a brother. That, or she was an excuse to lure Elizabeth into early morning meetings that might end with a seduction.

"You are unconvinced," Mr. Darcy observed.

"I am concerned."

"I do not know how to prove myself to you other than through my actions."

Elizabeth strove to drive the worry from his countenance with a smile. "Then it is your actions I shall observe, although I require an explanation of one more. How did you get the note here? I can't imagine you describing this location to anyone."

"I couldn't risk it, even if I could describe it. I came myself, of course. Colonel Fitzwilliam was in town and said he would spend the day with Georgiana. He took her to visit his sister, Lady Amanda. She has a daughter, Lady Sophia, who is now fifteen, Georgiana's age."

"Lady Amanda?" Elizabeth repeated, surprised. "Your cousin is titled?"

Mr. Darcy grimaced, looking as if he wished to call back the information. "My cousin, the one who would take partial custody of Georgiana, is an earl. The Earl of Matlock. That is why if there is any disagreement between me and him, a court would be likely to side with him."

Was his seeming reluctance to claim kinship to an earl real, or a ruse so he could hope to impress her without seeming to put himself forward? "Lady Amanda was in town during the summer?" Elizabeth wanted to believe him, but it was an odd time for a titled lady to be in London.

"She is coming to the end of mourning for her deceased husband and was replenishing her wardrobe. It was perfect, as I am ill equipped to help Georgiana with shopping. I told everyone I was tired of London and wanted to spend a day in the country. I had already arranged for horses."

"Your coachman must wonder why you took a fifty-mile round trip without spending any time here before heading back."

"I rode. Unfortunately, it took me almost an hour to find this place after I reached Netherfield Park."

Elizabeth sought for any flaws in his explanations. "You said your arranged for horses. Where from?"

He appeared amused by the question, obviously aware she tested him. "The horse I rode here was rented from and returned to Hoddesdon." Hoddesdon was four or five miles south of Meryton. "When I got back there, I rode the horse I'd left in Hoddesdon back to where I'd left Trafalgar. He was fed and well rested by the time I mounted him again."

"But you weren't?" Elizabeth said smilingly.

"Weren't what?"

"Fed and well rested."

"I was neither. But I returned in time, so they accepted that I had gone for a ride. Trafalgar wasn't overly tired."

"I'm glad to hear he's well," she said while she mused on Mr. Darcy's answers. He had them ready, which she deemed suspicious, but he spoke with enough detail that she was inclined to accept them. His candid expression gave her hope he spoke the truth. Their talk moved on to wider things. His tenants, for apparently, he possessed an estate in Derbyshire called Pemberley. Her family, both near and far. Their thoughts on the war in which his cousin must fight. By the time Elizabeth recalled she must return or suffer great suspicion, she felt well reassured.

Mostly.

She returned home to her normal day, which seemed oddly hollow after the forest, golden morning sunlight slanting across Mr. Darcy's face. The rumble of his voice as they conversed. How he stood so near, so obviously drawn to her and desirous of her touch, but kept his hands clasped behind his back…except for those brief, wonderful moments when he captured hers.

For the next several weeks, they acted aloof in public but often met in private. They agreed to try to meet on Saturdays and Mondays as well. At his suggestion, she selected a new meeting place, a delightful little dell snuggly between two forested ridges, only a walk of ten minutes from her home. His concern about her walking so far so often touched her, though she resolved to ensure he knew she wouldn't tolerate a man being overly protective.

When they met anywhere else, Mr. Darcy never offered even a hint of the man he showed her when they spoke in secret. Anyone observing them would note the cool, barely civil nature of their exchanges. Though his dedication to the ruse impressed her, done as it was for his sister, it also pained her. From their talks, she ascertained his deep dislike of pretense. As she came to know him better, she could read the strain of their every public encounter. She could tell that, each time he hid his feelings for her, it hurt him. She didn't like to see Mr. Darcy hurt.

Chapter Six

Drenched, for rain had caught them on their ride, Darcy returned to Netherfield with Bingley to find Miss Jane Bennet had fallen ill while visiting Bingley's sisters. In most other women, Miss Bennet's claim to be too sick to return home would have been pretense, but even Miss Bingley had to agree it was not. Bingley called for his carriage, changed, and went to fetch the apothecary.

The following morning, Miss Bennet still abed and unlikely to rise from it anytime soon, Elizabeth appeared. From her damp boots, beguiling flush and muddy hem, it was obvious she'd walked the three miles from Longbourn, and she looked enchanting. Darcy could hardly conceal his pleasure. He dared to flatter himself with the idea that concern for her sister wasn't the only impetus for her presence.

Yet she disappeared into her sister's room and did not come out, and Darcy knew fresh agony. To have Elizabeth so near yet be unable to go to her...But he could not. Miss Bennet obviously needed Elizabeth, and they still had to pretend, especially since Mr. Hurst was there.

Elizabeth did join them for dinner but when dinner was over, she returned directly to Miss Bennet. With so few of them, the men did not retreat for brandy nor the women for chatter, instead all five of them heading to their favored parlor. Darcy waited for the two sisters to sit together, then sat away from them, Bingley and Hurst taking places more in the middle of the room.

"How long do you suppose we'll be made to endure Miss Elizabeth?" Miss Bingley said. "Her manners are so atrocious as to ruin my enjoyment of the meal, and between her pride and impertinence, she had no conversation." Miss Bingley shook her head in mock sorrow. "And her gowns? Has she ever even been to London? Not that even the most established modiste could do anything to make someone as plain as Miss Elizabeth into a beauty."

Darcy looked away, attempting to hide his displeasure.

"No, I daresay not," Mrs. Hurst said. "No seamstress could. In truth, Miss Elizabeth has nothing to recommend her, but being an excellent walker. I shall never forget her appearance this morning. She really looked almost wild."

Miss Bingley delightfully picked up that thread. She and Mrs. Hurst exchanged insults to Elizabeth, who was not even present to defend herself. Darcy gripped the chair arms tightly and maintained his silence.

"Your picture may be very exact, Louisa," said Bingley, finally curtailing their venom. "But this was all lost upon me. I thought Miss Elizabeth Bennet looked remarkably well, when she came into the room this morning. Her dirty petticoat quite escaped my notice."

Miss Bingley turned to face Darcy, to his dismay. "You observed it, Mr. Darcy, I am sure, and I am inclined to think that you would not wish to see your sister make such an exhibition."

Forcing out the words expected of him, Darcy said, "Certainly not."

Thus encouraged, Miss Bingley rose from the settee she shared with her sister and crossed to take the chair beside him, where she continued issuing insults. Darcy wondered that she couldn't see how low and unappealing her behavior made her.

Finally, she issued in a half whisper, "I am afraid, Mr. Darcy, that this adventure has rather affected your admiration of her fine eyes."

Darcy could hold his tongue no longer. "Not at all," he replied; "they were brightened by the exercise."

This brought on a slightly stunned silence and he knew he'd admitted too much. How he wished he'd never uttered a word to Miss Bingley about Elizabeth's eyes. Not that they weren't fine, but because he'd missed his goal and given Miss Bingley fodder.

He'd tried to make Miss Bingley, who'd caught him staring over long at Elizabeth, believe he felt merely an aesthetic appreciation, not love. His words had done no good, and the deceit wrenched at him. He did not know how much longer he could keep up such ongoing pretense. The act seemed vitally necessary for Georgiana's future, but he abhorred it.

In the hope he would not have to prevaricate further, he attempted not to listen as the sisters continued their waspish criticism of Elizabeth. Bingley, at least, rose to her defense. Darcy only wished he could as well.

But he could not. Nor could he block out a conversation taking place before him. He could feel the eyes of Miss Bingley and Mrs. Hurst studying him as they spoke. Dissecting his reactions. He mustered the will to bolster his ruse before Mrs. Hurst imparted any suspicions to her husband, to be included in his letters.

As time passed, Miss Bennet improved. Elizabeth spent more time out of her sister's chamber, and Darcy continually sought her. He couldn't help himself. When they met alone, in secret, he need only keep his hands firmly clasped behind him to stay his impulses. But together at Netherfield, clasped hands were no good at preventing him from speaking with her.

To her credit, Elizabeth kept up their pretense well. Whether they talked about accomplishments or letter writing, she managed to find ways to disagree with him. It enchanted him that she was clever enough to allow them to talk, yet not appear to agree on anything.

But it was more than that. He hoped she would continue to challenge his statements when they were married. He was tired of the Miss Bingleys of the world, whose agreement with every opinion he voiced was, in fact, an insult. To agree with someone completely implied they were so closed minded that they couldn't listen to another viewpoint. Such agreement also suggested a fear that the other person would be insulted to be disagreed with, which would limit them and make it difficult for them to understand the world. It was natural to enjoy the company of those people who agreed with you, but those who pretended to agree were at best, false friends.

Darcy, seated at the writing desk while he thought on this, wished he could know Elizabeth's opinion. Unable to ask her with the others in the room, he had to be content guessing what she would think of his assessment of sycophants and false friends. Would she value politeness more than truth? He expected she would say it depended on the situation.

A shadow fell across the desk. Darcy looked up to see Miss Bingley. With a lack of haste, for that would garner attention, he rearranged the pages of his letter to hide a particular line. Earlier, before Miss Bingley joined them, Darcy had shown the page to Elizabeth, with his finger pointing to a sentence with her name in it.

"You write uncommonly fast," Miss Bingley said, to his vexation.

Hoping to dissuade her from conversation, he replied, "You are mistaken. I write rather slowly."

Inured to his displeasure, Miss Bingley proceeded to torment him with her advances. This devolved into a conversation with the entire room, in which Darcy's torment grew. Finally, Elizabeth intervened and saved him. Darcy cast her a grateful look and turned to finish his letter to Georgiana.

The following day, Darcy sat in the parlor with the others, as far from Elizabeth as the room permitted, and pretended to read. He longed to sit closer to her but feared to come too near. Without conscious thought, he might reach to touch her. To take her hand in his.

He realized he no longer looked at the book he held, but rather watched Elizabeth. He couldn't help darting a glance Miss Bingley's way. She watched him with narrowed eyes. Standing, she crossed to sit near him and, securing his attention, proceeded to obliquely criticize Elizabeth.

Darcy didn't openly disagree with her, but he wondered if Miss Bingley knew how much she revealed about herself with these criticisms. Not that it mattered. What mattered was not having to listen to Miss Bingley anymore.

To that end, he waited for her to pause and said, "Miss Bingley, may I prevail upon you for some music?"

Delight shone in her gaze. "Always, Mr. Darcy." She rose and moved to the pianoforte.

Darcy wished she truly meant always. Miss Bingley playing was much more bearable than Miss Bingley talking. It didn't help that her increased attention was his fault. He'd made her suspicious, causing her to increase the intensity of her pursuit.

Not wanting to give Miss Bingley more fodder, Darcy started avoiding interaction with Elizabeth, painful as that proved. Taking his cue, she obliged. Darcy felt quite certain it made them both miserable.

Meeting her in a deserted hall one afternoon after changing for dinner, Darcy halted. A quick glance showed no one about. He caught her hand, her touch alleviating much of the pain he'd endured the past several days.

Voice low, he advised, "Miss Bingley is suspicious. I'm trying to express no more than a casual interest in you. I'm sorry if I've been offending you."

Elizabeth squeezed his hand tightly. "I'm the one who should apologize. I've acted like I am trying to offend you. I hope I haven't succeeded in doing so."

"Never. I only admire you more. You are very clever." He caught her other hand, aware that he shouldn't, but unable to resist.

An impish smile livened her features. "It's fun, in a way, and I think we must be succeeding."

Darcy shook his head. "I don't believe we are."

"No? But I've accused you of implacable resentment and you've accused me of lying. How could Miss Bingley possibly think we care about each other?"

"Because she is not as wrapped up in herself as she sometimes seems," Darcy said. "She is catching nuances that go beyond words."

Elizabeth studied his eyes. "Do you really think she can tell how I feel about you?"

His heart pounded. "How do you feel about me?"

"As if I'd like to do this." She rose onto her tiptoes.

Footsteps sounded on the bottom steps of the staircase. Elizabeth's eyes, which had fallen half closed, flew wide. Releasing his hands, she ducked into her sister's room.

Darcy stood immobile, so shocked at nearly receiving Elizabeth's kiss, and then having the moment stolen, that he couldn't move. He opened his hands wide, then clenched his fists. Just as a head became visible on the staircase, he propelled himself forward.

Chapter Seven

Shortly after Elizabeth and Jane returned home, their father announced, in his usual chaos-inducing manner, that their cousin would visit. None of them had met the gentleman, a Mr. Collins, who proved a silly, taxing man. Worse, he'd come there to wed one of them. With immediacy and predictability, he set his sights on Jane, only to be firmly dissuaded by Mrs. Bennet, because she expected Jane to marry Mr. Bingley.

In an effort to mitigate the annoyance of Mr. Collins, they took him walking down into Meryton, where they were introduced to a rather dashing gentleman named Mr. Wickham. While talking to him, Mr. Darcy and Mr. Bingley rode up. Mr. Bingley, with even greater predictability than Mr. Collins, immediately applied his attention to Jane.

Amused, Elizabeth cast about, wondering if anyone would speak to her. Even though she knew he would not, at least not in public, she stole a glance at Mr. Darcy, only to find him watching her intently. She gave a miniscule shake of her head to indicate he should look elsewhere.

Mr. Darcy looked away from her, then turned white, eyes glinting with suppressed emotion.

Elizabeth followed his gaze to find his attention locked on their newest acquaintance, Mr. Wickham, who had gone red. Elizabeth took this in with fascination. Obviously, something stood between the two, but what? And how? One a gentleman from Derbyshire, the other a Lieutenant in the militia. The two took a barely cordial leave of each other, consigning Elizabeth to wonder the remainder of the day.

The following morning, the incident came back to her as she hurried to meet Mr. Darcy. With careful steps, Elizabeth followed the path she'd made into the dell. A gloomy sky let in little sunlight, even for morning, but by now, she could conjure the way to mind so well, she needed hardly any light.

A dark shape deep in the dell resolved into Mr. Darcy as she approached. He crossed the leaf and branch strewn valley floor, hands stretched out to take hers. Elizabeth, who'd long since abandoned wearing gloves to their meetings, reveled in the feel of his large warm hands about hers. In how his skin, though smooth, still seemed rougher than her own, especially as his thumbs caressed the backs of her hands.

"I believe Mondays and Wednesdays grow further apart in time," he said, gazing down at her.

He never did more than hold her hands. Sometimes, the way he looked at her, Elizabeth half hoped, and half feared, that he might. "I daresay, if they had, the world would notice."

He raised an eyebrow. "Do not tell me you don't feel the same way. That would score me."

She couldn't help but smile, her insides fluttering with his touch. "Mondays and Wednesdays are separated by an eternity."

"I suspected as much." He fell silent, gaze scouring her face in the half-light. Sometimes he would do that. Stare at her as if memorizing her, until her knees felt week.

But there was something that Elizabeth wished to know. This morning, she did not wish to become lost in Mr. Darcy's gaze. His behavior of the day before had been too odd. "Along with the strange disparity of time gripping Hertfordshire, I couldn't help but observe another phenomenon. It seemed to me you know this Lieutenant Wickham, and dislike him excessively."

His thumbs stilled their slow caress of her hands. "I do not wish to discuss Mr. Wickham."

"You know I cannot help but be intrigued and, after all, we agreed to these meetings to come to know each other." She squeezed his hands. "I know you well enough now that you must imagine there is little you could tell me about your relationship to the man that would color my opinion of you."

Mr. Darcy's eyes took on a flinty look she'd never seen directed at her, and only witnessed the day before, when he met Mr. Wickham. "Wickham and I grew up together. Since, we've fallen out." He scowled, just as he was wont to do in public. "That is all I have to say on the matter."

Here was a side of Mr. Darcy she'd never seen in private. She tugged her hands from his. "I see. We are permitted to speak on many things, including your sometimes uncharitable views of my family—"

"With which you generally agree," he interrupted.

"Which I tolerate and try to understand from your perspective," she corrected. "Yet, when I, for the first time, touch on a subject you find disagreeable, you declare it closed, as if your word is akin to the king's."

Mr. Darcy stared at her, silent.

After what seemed even more an eternity than the wait between Monday and Wednesday had, Elizabeth's insides twisting tighter the whole time, she managed an unconcerned shrug. If Mr. Darcy truly meant to marry her, he'd best understand that she would not be dictated to. "Hopefully you'll be less despotic on Saturday," she said and, turning on her heels, walked away.

Her every sense cried out against leaving him. She strained for any sound. For his footfalls coming after her. For his voice calling her back. So far as she could tell, for she refused to look, he did not move.

Let him stay there, then, she stormed inwardly. Let him be a statue until Saturday. That would give him time to think.

Unfortunately, it also gave her time to think, and she felt well and truly miserable by the time she, her sisters and Mr. Collins headed to Meryton for an evening at their aunt and uncle's. Many of their acquaintances also attended, including officers of the regiment. Among these was Mr. Wickham, to whom every female eye turned when he entered the room. He was so handsome, and so clearly sought after, Elizabeth couldn't help but smile when he came to sit beside her.

Over the course of the evening, Mr. Wickham informed Elizabeth that he was acquainted with the Darcys. Then, with compelling mischief in his eyes, he told her a story about Mr. Darcy denying him an income. Mr. Wickham spoke with affection of Mr. Darcy's late father and the man's dreams for him, which Mr. Darcy had denied. Mr. Wickham also declared Mr. Darcy's sister a great snob, worse than Miss Bingley.

Elizabeth's mind went to the line Mr. Darcy had shown her in a letter to his sister. 'When you meet her, you will like a woman I met here, Miss Elizabeth Bennet.' *When* you meet her, not *if*. But Mr. Darcy could have brought his sister with him to Hertfordshire. From comments made by his companions, they obviously knew and liked Miss Darcy. Did Mr. Darcy mean that line in his letter, or did it cover a desire to keep Elizabeth away from his relations?

Later, returned to Longbourn and readying for bed, Elizabeth ran a brush through her hair, considering the two men. Mr. Darcy had attempted nothing untoward. If he didn't love her, didn't wish to wed her, what possible motive could he possess for meeting her in secret? He seemed to enjoy her conversation, but that was hardly reason enough. He could just as easily converse with her in public.

He claimed to be upright, honest and all things good, but had carried on secret meetings with her for weeks, all the while making sure nothing could come back on him. Like as not, no one would believe Elizabeth if she chose to confess. Mr. Darcy wouldn't suffer, and her reputation would be tarnished by her own rumor.

And Mr. Wickham, all affability charm, showed equal inconsistency. He said he wouldn't defame Mr. Darcy because of the respect he had for Mr. Darcy's father, laudable behavior. Yet, Mr. Wickham then told her about Mr. Darcy's ill treatment of him, when he hardly knew her. Were she a gossip, he'd be spreading defamation indeed.

She wished desperately to believe Mr. Darcy was the more honest and upright of the two men, but could she afford to ignore the doubts Mr. Wickham raised? Her reputation, her entire future and those of her sisters, could be at stake. She knew she behaved horribly by sneaking off to meet Mr. Darcy. She hoped her faith placed well enough to avoid the dire consequences that might accompany her actions. If she decided the wrong man was true, she'd have long years to regret her acts.

Elizabeth felt no nearer an answer that Saturday when she rose before dawn and slipped out to meet Mr. Darcy again. A light rain fell, the prospect of the dell's shelter hurrying her steps more than the idea of seeing Mr. Darcy. Recalling how distant he'd become last time they met, she dreaded the questions she knew she must ask. Hood up against the drizzle, she crept down among the trees.

He waited, as he always did. He proffered hands gloved against the chill, but she held back, clutching her cloak closed. His touch, even through two sets of gloves, could rob her of her resolve to learn the truth. She couldn't forever be blind to Mr. Darcy's faults and keep, day by day, falling more in love with him.

"I spoke more with Mr. Wickham," she stated.

Though always upright, Mr. Darcy's stance became noticeably more rigid. "And?"

"He had some unflattering things to say about you. More than that, actually. According to him, you've behaved reprehensibly."

"According to George Wickham?" Vitriol dripped from Mr. Darcy's tone.

"That is what I said," Elizabeth replied, confused. Yes, she'd begun confrontationally, but not with accusation. "I would like to learn the truth."

"We've met here for weeks."

Elizabeth tipped her head to the side. "I am aware."

"Weeks with me, yet a few conversations with Wickham turn you against me."

"I am not turned against you. I've come seeking your side of things. It is my deepest hope to hear that I am a fool for giving Mr. Wickham even the courtesy of listening."

Mr. Darcy offered a brittle laugh. "No. I am the fool." He tipped his hat. "Good day, Miss Elizabeth. I don't suppose we shall meet like this again."

He started to turn, and she cried, "You are being unreasonable."

Mr. Darcy paused, face a silhouette against the murky predawn light. "What is unreasonable is that I fooled myself into believing I'd found someone who understands me. I should have realized you would be easily swayed. After all, I prevailed upon you to meet me in secret."

"I believe I suggested our secret meetings," she corrected. She drew in a deep breath and modulated her tone from annoyed to beseeching. "Please, simply tell me that Mr. Wickham has lied. Tell me that you are true, even though you agreed to meet me like this."

Mr. Darcy's profile angled toward the ground for a moment. He turned back to her, saying, "I am true. Whatever Mr. Wickham told you is a lie."

Elizabeth wanted desperately to believe him, but he sounded so odd. So much strain filled his voice. "Why do you hate the man so?"

Mr. Darcy shook his head. "His transgressions are many, but the incident which spurs me to hatred is a matter for family alone. You are not yet family."

"You are saying that to discover this secret, I must wed you?"

"I am."

Elizabeth stared at him incredulously. "You ask me to trust you without trusting me. You tell me you are in the right but refuse to explain why until I am irrevocably bound to you. Surely, you must see how perilous that seems?"

Mr. Darcy offered a shrug. "Think on it, then. As always, I will not pressure you." He angled his face toward the sky for a moment. "If it's raining like this on Monday, I won't bother to come."

He turned away again. This time, Elizabeth made no move to call him back. Quite stunned by his behavior, she simply stood there and watched him walk away.

Chapter Eight

It not only rained on Monday, but stormed. Elizabeth sat alone in the bedroom she shared with Jane, staring out the small window. Large, sleet filled droplets smacked the pane. Fancifully, she permitted a moment of sorrowful reverie, imagining the sky wept for her lost love.

Her lips quirked in a slight smile as, even through the pain Mr. Darcy's behavior evoked, she saw the silliness of her thoughts. The sky weeping indeed. Nothing existed to weep over. Mr. Darcy may have behaved foolishly, but the more Elizabeth thought on it, the more determined she became to mend the rift between them.

This stemmed in part from a determined analysis of both Mr. Darcy and Mr. Wickham. The latter, with his abundance of charm, struck her as someone for whom life came easily. A man who could talk his way into or out of any situation. She could readily imagine that every skill Mr. Wickham possessed and liberally employed came to Mr. Darcy with great difficulty, or not at all. Growing up together, the comparison would have been as unavoidable as comparing her sisters to one another and had likely often turned out in Mr. Wickham's favor. Mr. Darcy must be painfully accustomed to Mr. Wickham winning everyone's regard.

Unable to see Mr. Darcy that Monday or predict an end to the rain he'd employed as an excuse to remain away, Elizabeth determined she would confront him again at the ball Mr. Bingley had agreed to hold. There, she hoped to dance with Mr. Darcy. Surely, their need for secrecy wouldn't keep them from one set together. He would be clever enough to dance with others to conceal their attachment. His willingness to partner more than Miss Bingley and Mrs. Hurst could be explained by his courtesy to his host.

Determination filling her, Elizabeth joined in her sisters' preparations for the ball. On Tuesday, when the eve of the event arrived, they all piled into the carriage to ride to Netherfield Park. As they drew near, she entertained herself with the hope that she would dance both the opening dance and the supper dance with Mr. Darcy and be permitted to dine by his side.

"Cousin Elizabeth," Mr. Collins said as they all entered the room to greet their host. "Will you honor me with the first set?"

Elizabeth contained a grimace and replied, "Certainly."

Moments later, looking about as Mr. Collins led her into place, Elizabeth observed Mr. Darcy standing up with Miss Bingley. As duty demanded he partner first her then Mrs. Hurst, Elizabeth realized her aspiration of dancing with Mr. Darcy immediately had been a mere dream. She could not truly hope for the supper dance either, as she wished to partner him as soon as possible and her idea of two dances had also been a fanciful one. Entertaining to contemplate, but unlikely to come true.

Instead of the partner she wanted, Elizabeth stood with Mr. Collins and waited. The music began just as Mr. and Mrs. Hurst reached the floor, the musicians striking up a quadrille. Dancing with Mr. Collins proved excruciating. His steps slow, he held Elizabeth's hand too tightly. His conversation consisted of apologies for dancing improperly and praise of his home and neighbor. Horrified, Elizabeth realized he hoped to marry her, his accolades for his parsonage an attempt to win her over through social and financial standing.

Her set with Mr. Collins finally over, Elizabeth watched Mr. Darcy lead Mrs. Hurst out. Seeking to recover from having her toes trod on numerous times, Elizabeth started in the direction of her mother, only to be cut off by Miss Bingley and a stranger wearing the uniform of a colonel in the regulars.

"Miss Elizabeth," Miss Bingley gushed in a way that immediately put Elizabeth on guard. "A moment." She turned to the men at her side. "Colonel Fitzwilliam, this is the young lady about whom I was telling you, Miss Elizabeth Bennet. Miss Elizabeth, Colonel Fitzwilliam has only recently arrived in Hertfordshire."

Elizabeth worked to hide her surprise at the name. Colonel Fitzwilliam. Mr. Darcy's cousin who needed to sign off on his half of Miss Darcy's guardianship before Elizabeth and Mr. Darcy could announce their mutual admiration. Was he not meant to be heading to the continent soon?

The colonel, not ill-favored, bowed to her. "Miss Elizabeth. I've heard much about you. I believe we're too late for this set, but may I have the next?"

Elizabeth stole a glance at Mr. Darcy, who now danced with Mrs. Hurst. She wished to remain free for him to ask, but now could not. She cast Miss Bingley a suspicious look. Miss Bingley's expression shone with innocent pleasantness. Elizabeth turned back to the colonel. "I'd be delighted, sir."

While they waited for the next set to begin, the three of them chatted about the inconsequential. Miss Bingley largely stayed in the background. Colonel Fitzwilliam was obviously educated and well informed. Elizabeth enjoyed his conversation but didn't know what to make of finding him there. Why had he come? To see Mr. Darcy? To evaluate her? If he didn't know about her, why approach her so quickly?

Before the set concluded, Miss Bingley excused herself. As she departed, Colonel Fitzwilliam said, "Miss Bingley has been singing your praises so much that I had to dance with you. I want to get to know you."

His words threw Elizabeth's thoughts into a jumble. When Miss Bingley was far enough away so that she probably couldn't overhear, Elizabeth found her voice with one word, awash in sarcasm, "Really?"

"Yes, really." Colonel Fitzwilliam glanced at Miss Bingley's retreating back and quietly said, "She thinks my wanting to get to know you will remove a rival."

Elizabeth's stomach fell. So he did know. He really was there to evaluate her. Her mind raced back over their conversation thus far. Had she said anything terribly untoward?

Colonel Fitzwilliam held out an arm and led her to the dance floor. Elizabeth's thought continued their tumultuous flips. Colonel Fitzwilliam knew about her and Mr. Darcy. At least some of it. She had no idea as to how much. She had to be careful.

But he didn't make it difficult for her. They spoke pleasantly about impersonal topics. He was charming in a way Mr. Wickham wasn't. Mr. Wickham's charm was related to a deliberate attempt to please. Colonel Fitzwilliam's charm was based on the type of person he was.

After the second dance of their set, he led her to a quiet corner of the room. With a bow, he whispered, "I look forward to calling you cousin. And I am certainly not a rival to Darcy, since a few days ago I became engaged to a widow with no money and two children." Straightening, he smiled affably. "In other words, a much worse match than Darcy is considering."

With that, Colonel Fitzwilliam strode off, heading in the direction of a group of unpartnered young women. Elizabeth remained where he'd left her, stunned. Colonel Fitzwilliam, it seemed, knew everything. And he approved. Was that approval enough to grant Mr. Darcy full custody over his sister?

Her thoughts roiled so, Elizabeth couldn't have said how many sets had passed when she saw Mr. Darcy approaching. Her heart leapt, but her mind rebelled. Reaching her, he bowed.

"Will you dance with me, Miss Elizabeth?"

Her nod a bit shaky, she accepted his hand.

At first, she permitted herself to simply enjoy the dance, without saying a word. Elizabeth found Mr. Darcy remarkably proficient for one who claimed dislike of the activity. To dance with him there, in that grand ballroom with festivities all about, was all she'd ever dreamed of.

Yet that was a lie. She dreamed of much more. Mustering her courage, she said, "We attempted a conversation that went quite badly. I believe we should start again."

Hope touched his features. "I should like that. I did not do an admirable job of it the first time. I feared you would not speak with me again."

"I am more steadfast than that." Elizabeth smiled. "And more stubborn." She drew in a long breath and said, referring to the day in Meryton as if their last secret meeting hadn't taken place, "When you met us there the other day, we had just been forming a new acquaintance."

The effect was immediate. A deeper shade of hauteur overspread his features, but he said not a word, and Elizabeth, though blaming herself for her own weakness, could not go on. At length Darcy spoke, and in a constrained manner said, "Mr. Wickham is blessed with such happy manners as may ensure his making friends—whether he may be equally capable of retaining them, is less certain."

Her relief, she imagined, must rival his, for she'd known an excruciating moment of fear that this conversation would progress as badly as the first. Forcing a light tone, she replied, "I admit I found him charming at first, but I was struck by some inconsistencies in what he said."

"Thank goodness," Darcy said. "I would hate to lose you to his lies…or my obstinance. What did he tell you?"

"He said you withheld a living from him that he should have received after your father's death."

"I suspect he did not explain that at his request, I paid him three thousand pounds for the rights to the living. Colonel Fitzwilliam will confirm that."

Elizabeth shook her head. "There is no need for confirmation. Mr. Wickham also told me that he wasn't afraid of meeting you, but he isn't here. It seems that he is not only a liar, but a bad liar."

Darcy offered a grimace. "No, Wickham wouldn't dare show his face here. Especially with Colonel Fitzwilliam present."

"Your cousin dislikes Mr. Wickham as well?"

"Exceedingly."

Elizabeth narrowed her gaze. "You both dislike him, yet only you grew up with him." She hesitated but couldn't stifle her curiosity, or the desire to know if she guessed aright. "Does your joint hatred of him have ought to do with your joint guardianship of Miss Darcy and your poor decision?"

Darcy stared at her for so long, and with such intensity, Elizabeth began to fear she'd angered him again. Finally, he offered a quiet chuckle. "One of the things that draws me to you is your intelligence."

"That is not an answer."

"It most certainly is, but not a full one. You cannot have that yet." His expression warmed. "You do not know how much it means to me that you do not believe Mr. Wickham."

"He has obviously lied."

"Yet he has a history of being believed."

"I guessed as much." Elizabeth returned Darcy's smile, but then concern reasserted itself. "How much does Colonel Fitzwilliam know about us?"

"Everything."

"How can this be?"

"I called him here and confessed all." Darcy's hand tightened on hers, the sensation sending a thrill through her.

"How can this be?" Darcy had made the consequence of his cousin finding out about them seem so very dire. "What changed?"

"Colonel Fitzwilliam's mind."

"How?"

"His sister changed it."

Letting a touch of exasperation color her tone, Elizabeth said, "I think that requires an explanation, sir."

"Did I tell you his sister, Lady Amanda, was married at sixteen? Her brother, the earl, pushed her into a marriage she didn't want. She was widowed a little over a year ago."

"I'm sorry to hear that," Elizabeth murmured, recalling he'd before stated that she'd recently come out of mourning and knowing that, eventually, Darcy would come to the point.

He nodded in acknowledgment of her solicitude. "I believe I mentioned she has a daughter Georgiana's age?"

"Yes. Lady Sophia."

Darcy appeared pleased. "You remember."

Elizabeth smiled up at him, not caring if anyone watched them. "I make a point of attending to everything you say, Mr. Darcy."

He stared at her, gaze traversing her features.

"And you were saying?" Elizabeth prodded.

"Oh. Yes." After a pause, he continued. "The earl, Matlock, suggested a match for Sophia, a philandering widower with a title. When Lady Amanda refused and Matlock tried to insist, she apparently told him, Colonel Fitzwilliam and Sophia what her marriage had been like. In careful, painful and sordid detail."

Elizabeth's eyes went wide. "Oh dear. She said all that in front of her daughter?"

Darcy nodded, appearing amused rather than scandalized. "Matlock and Richard reportedly protested that part, but Lady Amanda said, 'She absolutely must hear this. When she is being bullied to accept a marriage she does not want, she should know what mine was like. I want her to have the strength I didn't have.' Apparently, hearing his sister's story persuaded Colonel Fitzwilliam I can do no worse for Georgiana than his brother will."

Elizabeth returned Darcy's smile. "I think I'm going to like Lady Amanda."

"I hope so, because if I have my way, she will be your cousin as soon as I can arrange it."

Elizabeth's breath caught. She looked up at him expectantly.

"I've wanted to formally propose since the moment I met you, but it wasn't the right thing to do. Yesterday evening, Colonel Fitzwilliam arrived with the signed document ceding Georgiana's guardianship to me, providing he is not in England. Nothing will ever again keep me from you."

The dance ended. Darcy still stared down at her, her hands clasped in his. Elizabeth, feeling dizzy, tried to remember to breathe.

"I won't pressure you," Darcy said. "If you want to wait, I will wait, but I sent to London for a special license. I've loved you since we met and the more I see you, the more I love you. My patience is nearly exhausted. Will you marry me?"

"Yes," Elizabeth breathed. "The answer is yes."

"When?" Darcy asked eagerly.

Elizabeth grinned. "I'd say a special license sounds like a good idea."

"I will speak to your father," he said and finally relinquished her hands.

As he walked away, Elizabeth realized they'd garnered many looks. Her cheeks heated, but she couldn't suppress a smile. Let people whisper. Soon, she and Mr. Darcy would give them something they could do more than whisper about.

Elizabeth accepted a dance from an officer she knew slightly but she wasn't a good partner. At every turn, her gaze sought Darcy, tracking him about the room. She saw him speaking with her father, amused but pleased, and somewhat gratified, that he didn't wait for a more conventional time.

After her dance with the officer, her father approached her. He led her to the side of the room and said, "You've been carrying on with Mr. Darcy for how long?"

Elizabeth blushed. She'd considered the possible hard to her reputation, even her sisters', but not for a moment had she paused to consider how her father might view her strange courtship by Darcy.

As she tried to decide whether her first meeting constituted 'carrying on' and whether the long absence should be counted, her father said gently, "I watched the two of you dance. I've always wanted you to be happy, and you were radiant. You have my permission to marry him, if that is what you want."

"I want it so much that I would marry him tomorrow."

"That is a little precipitous."

"Do you insist on the banns being read?" she asked, not hiding her disappointment.

"No. But it is unlikely we will get to sleep before three in the morning. Thursday is the soonest I will allow it." He spoke in a firm tone, but humor sparked in his eyes. "In fact, I insist on Thursday. It has the advantage that your mother won't have time to spend too much money on the wedding. With any luck, she will sleep well past noon tomorrow."

Elizabeth chuckled. "Thursday it is, then."

"Your Mr. Darcy is very generous. He doesn't want a dowry and the amount he will settle on you will make Miss Bingley jealous. Your mother will boast of it for the next decade. Although I don't approve of how the courtship was handled, I cannot complain about the results."

Elizabeth's face reheated. She truly had behaved reprehensibly. "Papa, I—"

Her father waved her silent. With the ghost of a smile on his face, he said, "I suspect that Mrs. Bennet would never forgive me if I didn't give permission for you to get married, and I would hear her complain about it for the rest of my life." He looked past her, his smile turning wistful. "Here comes one with more to say to you than I have." Her father patted her on the arm and walked away.

Elizabeth turned to find Darcy approaching and, despite her father's sorrow, she could do nothing but smile.

Darcy remained by her side for the rest of the evening. His presence kept most men away, but Mr. Collins came up to them once and gave Darcy a long-winded justification of introducing himself on the pretext of providing information about Darcy's aunt. As he spoke, Mr. Collins kept looking at Elizabeth with a puzzled expression. Finally, to her relief, he left.

"What is bothering him?" Darcy asked.

"He decided he is going to marry me. I'm having trouble convincing him I am not interested."

"I should hope you aren't," Darcy exclaimed, voice edged with a growl.

The supper dance came, and Elizabeth had the exquisite pleasure of dancing again with the man she loved. She allowed all her hidden emotions to show, as did he. The love she saw on his face was worth all the secrecy and doubt.

At supper, Mrs. Bennet spoke of a marriage between Jane and Mr. Bingley as a settled thing, which it wasn't. She mentioned all the advantages of the marriage, including letting Jane's sisters meet rich men. Elizabeth, mortified, did all she could to avoid Darcy's gaze.

He touched her arm. Unable to stop herself, Elizabeth turned to look at him. They exchanged a glance. Suddenly, Elizabeth's embarrassment gave way to humor. Darcy must have caught the gleam in her eye. He stood up and said, "There is no need to give Elizabeth the chance to meet rich men. She has already consented to be my wife."

Mrs. Bennet's jaw dropped and for once, she was silent.

"But I expected…" Mr. Collins' voice tapered off. He muttered something about someone disapproving, but no one paid attention to him, least of all Darcy and Elizabeth.

Epilogue
Nine years later

Darcy watched the retreating carriage with mixed feelings. His children would miss their aunt and he would miss his sister. Georgiana, now a marchioness, was married and gone. The marriage had not been a grand affair befitting the rank of the groom, but only had guests who were genuinely close to Georgiana or her husband. Both were reserved and disliked crowds. Not even all of their friends had been able to attend. Jane and Charles Bingley weren't there because Jane had given birth to her third child a few days before the wedding. Bingley had sent word that he was delighted to have a son.

"We will see her often in London," Elizabeth said, echoing Darcy's thoughts about Georgiana. She wrapped an arm about his, leaning against his side.

"I hope so," Colonel Fitzwilliam said, on Darcy's other side. "Who would have thought she would marry so advantageously? My brother told me we were very clever to wait until she was twenty-four to let her wed, so she could catch a marquess."

"Yes, but he believed your marriage was strategically planned," Elizabeth teased. Colonel Fitzwilliam had promised a dying comrade that he would help his sister, who was an impoverished widow with two children. He fell in love and married her. Two years into the marriage, a cousin of hers died, leaving her a property that brought a good income.

"Yes, but my brother never believed I was happy before Emily's cousin died. He also assumed I knew the cousin would leave her everything. I didn't even know he existed."

"I'd only met him a handful of times, when we were young," Emily Fitzwilliam said with a smile. "If you'll excuse me, I should check on our little one."

"I'll join you," Colonel Fitzwilliam said. He offered her his arm, which she accepted. Together they retreated into Pemberley.

Darcy tugged his arm free of Elizabeth's, but only so he could wrap it about her shoulders. "That leaves me as the only one whose marriage Matlock disapproves of," Darcy said, looking fondly at his wife.

Elizabeth cast him a mischievous, challenging look. "Are you sorry to disappoint the earl?"

Darcy leaned close and whispered, "I wanted to marry you when we first met, and I've never once regretted that decision. Not even for a moment." Tugging her to him, he kissed her with a passion that would never dim.

~ The End ~

About the Authors

Renata McMann

Renata McMann is the pen name of Teresa McCullough, someone who likes to rewrite public domain works. She is fond of thinking, "What if?" To learn more about Renata's work and collaborations, visit www.renatamcmann.com.

Summer Hanford

Starting in 2014, Summer was offered the privilege of partnering with fan fiction author Renata McMann on her well-loved *Pride and Prejudice* variations. More information on these works is available at www.renatamcmann.com.

Summer is currently partnering with McMann as well as writing solo works in Regency Romance and Fantasy. She lives in New York with her husband and compulsory, deliberately spoiled, cats. The newest addition to their household is an energetic setter-shepherd mix…not yet appreciated by any of the three cats. For more about Summer, visit www.summerhanford.com.

Get Your Thank You Gift! Sign Up for Our Mailing List Today!

Visit: www.renatamcmann.com/news/

Manufactured by Amazon.ca
Bolton, ON